Driven
By Becky Durfee

Dedication

There are too many people to thank for their support. Everyone in my life has been encouraging when I've disclosed my previously-secret and still-embarrassing plight to write a book.

I will say these words would have never been put on paper if it weren't for the love and support of my wonderful husband Scott. When I mentioned I wanted to write a book, he simply said, "Go for it." I did, and now here I am.

My children and step-children have also been wonderful means of support. My daughter Julia routinely asked when my book was going to be published. When I replied, "Probably never," that wasn't a good enough answer for her. She encouraged me to get it published, or at least try, and I couldn't argue. How am I supposed to encourage my children to follow their dreams when I'm too afraid to follow mine? So thank you, Hannah Durfee, Seneca Durfee, Evan Fish and Julia Fish. You've been my inspiration.

More thanks to the people who read my book when it was a simple email attachment: LynDee Walker, Sam Travers and Felicia Underwood. Their positive comments gave me the courage to submit the book for publication. More thanks to Bill and Sarah Demarest for additional edits.

So many other people have touched my life in a way that has been reflected in this book. Again, there are too many to mention, but you all know who you are. ☺

Chapter 1

2013

"Everything hurts," Jenny said weakly.

Jenny Watkins lay on one end of the sofa; her husband Greg occupied the other. Exhaustion ravaged her body as she looked around the room at the countless boxes waiting to be unpacked, a thought she couldn't even begin to contemplate being as sore as she was. Loading the moving van at the old apartment in Kentucky had been easy for her; with all of their friends and family around to help out, she was tasked with minimal heavy lifting. Unloading in Evansdale, Georgia, however, had been a different story. Three hundred miles from home, they had no friends to help, so she found herself struggling with her end of a couch, some dressers, and various other items she hoped to never lift again.

Her eyes scanned the room, noting the peeling paint, antiquated fixtures, and inadequate lighting. Lifting furniture had been only step one in a very long process which, at that moment, invoked more dread in her than excitement. Flipping this once-beautiful house had seemed like a reasonable idea when Greg had first devised the plan; now she wasn't so sure.

At that moment an inexplicable wave of déjà vu washed over her. The feeling lasted only a couple of seconds before it vanished completely. Due to its brevity, she dismissed it as nothing more than exhaustion.

"Next time we're hiring movers," she muttered. "I hurt in places I didn't know I had."

"Teachers can't afford movers," Greg countered, throwing a pizza crust into the delivery box at the foot of the couch. "Besides, I don't know what you're complaining about. You only did about a quarter of what I did."

Jenny wished he was kidding, but she knew he wasn't. Even though she had lifted more than she'd ever thought possible, it still wasn't enough for Greg. Under ordinary circumstances that comment would have made her angry; at the moment, however, she didn't have enough energy to become irritated.

The two laid in silence as Jenny considered how difficult it had been to say goodbye to everyone back home. She'd spent her whole life in Kentucky. Most of her friends were there; her family was there. Over the past few months she'd spent so much time deciding on a house and applying for jobs in Georgia that she hadn't fully considered what she'd be sacrificing when she moved, which was essentially her entire life as she knew it. Apparently she'd underestimated the void she'd feel in her heart when she left it all behind.

In an attempt to thwart the tears that threatened to fall, Jenny stood up, groaning with pain. "I've got to go to bed," she announced warily. She put her hand on her forehead as a realization struck. "Which box has the sheets?"

"It's upstairs in the corner of the bedroom," Greg replied.

"Okay, thanks," Jenny said. She picked up the pizza box and held it out to Greg. "You done?"

"One more," Greg replied, taking a piece from the box. Jenny stopped by the kitchen to put the rest of the pizza in the refrigerator and then headed up to the bedroom. She said "Ow" precisely thirteen times on her way, once for every step in the stairwell. Upon reaching the bedroom she managed to locate the box that contained the sheets rather easily, but then she struggled to open it. Tape had never been so difficult to remove. Despite the fact that she felt like she had weights dangling from her limbs, she managed to put the fitted sheet on the mattress, which was lying on the floor in the center of the room. After successfully tucking the last corner in, she half-heartedly threw a comforter on top and declared, "Good enough." She headed into the bathroom, dutifully taking her toothbrush out of the toiletries bag.

5

She heard Greg come in as she was almost finished brushing her teeth. "I think I'm going to bed, too," he declared. "We've got a long day tomorrow."

Jenny spit into the sink. "I don't even want to think about it." She kissed his cheek as she walked past him and collapsed onto the mattress. Within seconds she felt waves of relaxation washing over her.

"Steve O'dell." The words woke her with a start.

"What?" She asked her husband, somewhat annoyed that he had woken her.

"I didn't say anything," he said, sliding onto the mattress next to her.

"I swear to God I heard you say a name," Jenny replied.

"Nope," Greg said. "You're hearing things, babe."

"Great. That's all I need." She wriggled in the bed, getting comfortable again. "Love you."

Greg leaned over and turned off the lamp. "Goodnight."

Jenny wondered exactly what it would take for her husband to ever say the words, "Love you too." With a shrug she dismissed the thought and fell asleep almost instantly.

She awoke to the sound of Greg unzipping a suitcase. "Hey," she said groggily, squinting at the brightness of the curtain-less room. "What time is it?"

Greg glanced at his watch. "6:45."

"It's early," Jenny wiped her eyes. "You sure you don't want to sleep a little longer?"

"Lots to do," he replied, putting on his clothes.

In Jenny's mind she knew she should have been getting out of bed too, but she just couldn't bring herself to do it. She closed her eyes, hearing the sounds of Greg getting ready to take on the day, finding herself both jealous of his enthusiasm and irritated by it. She drifted in and out of sleep as he made noise while getting ready, until she finally heard him head downstairs. The resulting quiet allowed her a few moments of deeper slumber.

"Steve O'dell."

Jenny shot up in bed. She distinctly heard a name; there was no denying it this time. She looked around the room to see if Greg had come back in, but she heard him milling around downstairs. She sat very still, scanning the room with just her eyes, consumed with the eerie feeling she wasn't alone.

"What is going on here?" she whispered as fear engulfed her body. "*Who is in this house?*"

Now wide awake, she hopped out of bed and quickly headed downstairs. "I heard it again," she immediately told Greg with a trembling voice. "I swear I just heard a man say 'Steve O'dell.' It's the same name I heard last night when I thought it was you."

Greg nonchalantly continued rummaging through a box. "Are you saying the place is haunted? Is that why we got it so cheap?"

Greg's calm reaction caused Jenny to realize how crazy she must have sounded. She let out a laugh as the fear left her body. "I guess you're right. I'm being ridiculous. I just don't know what's gotten into me."

Greg pulled some plates out of a box. "Did you do any drugs back in college that you didn't tell me about?" He glanced at her with a smirk.

"Yeah, right. I was a real party animal back then," she said sarcastically. She rubbed her temples. "Maybe I'm becoming schizophrenic."

"You're probably just tired," Greg reasoned, "or stressed out. Stress can do some funny things to people, and you're certainly under a lot of stress."

"I don't know," she declared, eager to change the subject. "How many plates are you unpacking?"

"I figure about four," he said. "A few cups and a little bit of silverware. That should get us through for a while. I hope to get the cabinets done before school starts, and then we can unpack the rest."

Jenny nodded in approval. She ran her fingers through her hair as she walked over to a box labeled "food," dragging it over to the pantry. She ripped off the tape, opened the box, and reluctantly began the daunting task of unpacking.

By the end of the day, the house had some semblance of order; Jenny and Greg were able to eat dinner at the kitchen table, which was actually located in the kitchen.

Jenny stirred the take-out Chinese food with her fork and looked around. "You know, this house must have been incredible in its day."

7

"No kidding," Greg agreed, "It's a shame it was let go like this. Well, not for us. We get to reap the benefits of somebody else's laziness."

Jenny wiped her forehead with the back of her hand. "It's hot in here. Are you sure the air conditioning is on?"

"It's on," Greg assured her, "but it's struggling. We're definitely going to have to upgrade that. The unit is too small to keep up with a house this size."

Jenny's expression reflected her disappointment; that was exactly the kind of thing she didn't want to spend time or money on. The artist in her wanted to jump straight to the cosmetic work. She viewed the house as a blank canvas, just like the ones she used to fill with intricate landscapes before she'd met Greg. Looking around the kitchen she envisioned paint on the walls, curtains on the windows and granite countertops complementing the new appliances. She smiled as she considered the house's aesthetic potential.

"I'm thinking a light mustard color in here," she announced.

Greg squinted. "Really? *Mustard*? I was thinking more of a tan color. Mustard may not be neutral enough."

Jenny made a face as she pictured the walls being tan. She didn't think that would have looked nearly as nice, but as she did with many things, she kept that opinion to herself.

"I feel like I've been hit by a bus," she exclaimed as she walked her empty take out containers to the trash can.

"We've only just begun," he said. "Look on the bright side; we don't need to spend money on a gym membership." He, too, threw out his containers.

"I'd better look like a model when this whole thing is over," she said dryly. "Can we call it a night as far as work goes? I'd love nothing more than to sit down on the couch and chill out for a while. I think I'm done unpacking for the day."

"Yeah, me too." Greg replied, stretching. "I think twelve hours is long enough." The two lumbered into the living room, plopped down on the couch, and started to watch television. Jenny did not last long, however; fatigue quickly got the better of her, and she declared she needed to go upstairs to bed.

Once upstairs she looked longingly at the mattress on the floor as she changed into her pajamas. She wished she could just climb into bed fully dressed with dirty teeth, but something within her would never allow that to happen. She needed to follow her routine.

After she'd completed her ritual, she laid down on the mattress. Within a couple of minutes she was drifting off to sleep. Then she heard it—that same unmistakable voice that had startled her twice before.

"Elanor Whitby."

Chapter 2

September, 1957

Elanor Whitby sat on a picnic blanket overlooking Lake Wimsat with her boyfriend Ronald Dwyer. He sat very close to her, his arm around her waist, looking out at the water. The trees around the lake were just starting to show hints of color, which made the view even more breathtaking. The temperature was ideal, the sun was shining and a light breeze was blowing. Ronald had planned everything else to a tee, arriving a half an hour before Elanor to make sure all of her favorite foods were on display when she arrived--the beautiful weather was the icing on the cake. Ronald couldn't have been happier; he knew this was Elanor's favorite place on earth, and everything was falling into place so nicely. Today was going to be absolutely perfect.

"I'm really glad we're able to spend the day together," he said. "I've been missing you lately. You sure have been spending a lot of time at the magazine."

"I know," Elanor replied apologetically, "but it's really starting to take off now. I'm getting quite a following." She smiled proudly, her blue eyes sparkling with excitement. "This little pet project of mine is turning out to be quite a hit."

"That's great," Ronald said unenthusiastically. He turned his body to face her, looking at her very seriously. "But have you ever thought about having something more?"

Elanor squinted in the sunlight. "More?"

"Yeah," he said, his voice reflecting increasing excitement. "Like a husband. A family. With lots of kids running around. You know, a normal life."

Elanor retracted at the statement. Sensing her apprehension, Ronald continued to argue his case. "You've been working awfully hard lately, with the long hours and all. I hate to see you having to work so much. I hardly get to see you anymore." He lowered his eyes. "I love you, Elanor, and I want to provide for you. I want you to be able to quit the magazine. I want it to be the two of us, all the time. You and me."

Elanor let out a sigh. "I love you too, Ronald. I truly do." She looked into his hopeful brown eyes and felt her heart split in two. "But I'm not doing the magazine because I feel like I have to. I'm doing it because I love it." She peered out at the lake, protecting Ronald from the optimism in her eyes. "I feel like I can make a difference. I want women to know there's a whole world out there. And based on the increasing popularity of the magazine, it's a message that women want to hear. Every month my readership gets bigger." She hugged her knees into her chest. "I'm actually very anxious to see how big this thing will get."

"But if the magazine gets any bigger, we won't see each other at all."

Elanor didn't say anything. It was a prospect she'd already considered. Ronald was a dear, sweet, hard-working boy with a baby face and a refreshing, childlike innocence. His heart, which he wore on his sleeve, was pure, and he'd never uttered a dishonest word in his life. However, he didn't offer her the intellectual stimulation she required. A life with Ronald would have indeed been simple and pleasant, but Elanor knew she needed something more. No matter how kind Ronald was, she would have never been happy just being somebody's wife.

Had Ronald ever read any of her articles, he would have known that about her.

Wary of her silence, but determined nonetheless, Ronald continued. "Elanor, you're the most beautiful woman I've ever met. Inside and out. You make me so happy. If you give me the chance, I promise I will do everything I can to make you happy, too." He reached into his pocket and pulled out a ring box. Opening it, and getting up onto one knee, he said, "Elanor Whitby, will you marry me?"

Time stood still for Elanor. She couldn't believe she had let it go this far. Time and time again she told herself that she needed to end the relationship, but she never felt the need was immediate. He was such a kind soul, and the thought of hurting him was such an unpleasant image she'd always decided to put it off for another day. But she had waited too long. Now here he was, kneeling before her with a ring in his hand, and the rejection was going to be a million times more painful than it needed to be.

"Oh, Ronald," she sighed, reaching out to touch his face. "You are an amazing man. Truly. But the life you describe..." she shook her head and reduced her voice to a sympathetic whisper, "it just isn't for me."

Ronald leaned back and distanced himself from Elanor. "So what are you saying?" His voice reflected both sadness and anger. "You're choosing the magazine over me? You'd rather live alone and work sixteen hours a day than be married to me?"

"Don't say it like that," she argued. "This magazine...it's a dream of mine. I need to see it through. If I give up on it now I'll spend the rest of my life wondering how big it could have gotten. How many women it could have helped."

"And you don't think you'll spend the rest of your life wondering how happy you could have been with me?" His voice cracked at the end of the question, and tears began to well up in his eyes.

The agony on Ronald's face was heartbreaking, but it didn't change the answer. A rock formed in the pit of Elanor's stomach as she acknowledged what she had to do. She closed her eyes so she wouldn't have to see the expression on his face when he heard the words. "I'm sorry, Ronald."

Ronald remained quiet and motionless for what seemed like an eternity, until he wordlessly closed the ring box and put it back in his pocket. He got up and began to throw all the carefully-planned food hastily back into the picnic basket.

Then the words started. "I don't believe this." He sniffed a few times and wiped the tears from his eyes. He walked over to Elanor and pointed at her as she sat motionlessly. "I've been good to you! I don't deserve this!"

"I agree," Elanor whispered, hanging her head. She resolved herself to hear anything he had to say, feeling deep down inside that she deserved every bit of it.

Ronald threw a few more items into the basket, and then returned to Elanor to add more. "I would have made a good husband! A *good* husband!"

"I know. And you will make a good husband…for the right woman."

"But you *are* the right woman! Aww, just forget it." He made a dismissive gesture with his hand and stormed off for his car, leaving Elanor and the blanket behind.

Elanor remained still for quite a while after he left, as if continuing to brace herself. Eventually the sound of the birds chirping and the light breeze relaxed her enough to abandon her statuesque demeanor and take a deep breath. She once again hugged her knees to her chest, looking out over the lake.

While she couldn't determine exactly what she was feeling, she was quite sure it wasn't the correct emotion. She should have been heartbroken considering her relationship just ended, but she felt strangely happy—relieved. She had been dreading this moment for a long time, and now it had passed. With Ronald out of the picture, she now had the ability to focus on the magazine without feeling like she was disappointing someone every minute she was there. With her dreams being what they were, deep down inside she knew she was better off without a man in her life bringing her down.

As she sat by herself, newly single, overlooking her favorite place in the world, she felt less alone than she had in years.

Chapter 3

2013

Jenny sat at the computer with her note pad, scribbling down information about any Steve O'dell she could find. None of it seemed to make any sense. A photographer from Texas, a lawyer in Wisconson…why on earth would she been hearing any of their names at a house in Evansdale, Georgia? She tried different variations of the name…Steve, Steven, Stephen…all to no avail. Confused but undeterred, she decided to switch gears and focus on Elanor Whitby.

A quick search yielded multiple results, all about the founder of *Choices* magazine. Jenny clicked on a biography, which stated that the magazine founder had been born in Evansdale in 1934. Jenny's blood ran cold. Finally there was a connection.

On a hunch Jenny went to the county website's real estate section to obtain an ownership history of her new house. She typed in her address, and the list of all of the property's owners appeared chronologically. The first names on the list were Luther and Mary Ellen Whitby, the original owners who lived in the house for 37 years.

"Oh my God," Jenny whispered. "Did she live here?"

Grateful for the information age, Jenny looked up free genealogy websites, locating multiple places she could look up family trees. After several failed attempts to find a site that was easy to use, she typed in the only information she had about Elanor—her name, birth date, and the town. Results popped up instantly.

Elanor Whitby, born in 1934, was the only child of Luther and Mary Ellen Whitby.

Jenny looked around the house, realizing that Elanor Whitby, founder of *Choices* magazine, had grown up there as a child. She had learned to walk on those very floors, gazed outside those windows, played tag in that back yard. Jenny wondered how the house had looked when Elanor lived there—what color the walls had been, how the furniture had been arranged.

And she wondered why Elanor's name, as well as the mysterious Steve O'dell, rang in her ears as she drifted off to sleep.

Excited about her new finding, she raced to find Greg, who was upstairs unpacking boxes. "You'll never guess what I've uncovered."

Greg didn't look up from the box he was sorting through. "Oh yeah?" he said unenthusiastically. "What?"

Undeterred by his lack of interest, she continued. "Elanor Whitby…that name I heard last night as I was falling asleep…she lived here as a child. Her parents were the original owners of this house."

"That's good," he said, closing up the box. "I guess your mystery's solved, then."

"My mystery's solved?" Jenny asked. She had believed this discovery only deepened the mystery.

"Yeah." Greg replied. "You must have seen her name written somewhere. On some document or something. Now, for whatever reason, you think you're hearing it." He walked past Jenny to the closet and put this box into storage with many others.

"I don't *think* I'm hearing it," Jenny said, turning to face him. "I *am* hearing it. Why are you so quick to dismiss this?" Her tone reflected a hint of annoyance.

"Because," he said, pausing to look her in the eye. "We have lots of work to do." He continued on to another box, opened it, and began rummaging through.

Jenny stood silently for a moment as she entertained the debate going on in her head. She certainly didn't appreciate Greg's lackluster reaction; however, she did have to acknowledge that she had been sitting at the computer for the past hour while Greg unpacked boxes by himself. She could see why he'd be irritated with her. Always eager to avoid a fight, Jenny grabbed a box and pulled off the tape.

They unpacked in silence for a while, until Jenny delicately announced, "I was thinking that I could try to find her."

"Who?" Greg asked. "That woman?"

"Yes. Elanor."

"Why?"

"I want to find out who Steve O'dell is." Jenny shrugged sheepishly. "Maybe somebody is trying to deliver a message to me. Maybe there's something I should be doing."

Greg didn't deliver an answer right away. He put away a few items from the box, and eventually said, "So you think *spirits* are talking to you or something?" His tone made her feel like a reprimanded child.

"I don't know," she confessed, "but I think it's worth investigating."

Greg didn't say anything, so Jenny continued. "According to the information I found, Elanor is still alive. She'd be in her early eighties now." Jenny took a few items out of her box. "She was the founder of *Choices* magazine, you know. She was quite a successful woman."

"That doesn't surprise me," Greg said. "Look at where she grew up. It seems success ran in her family."

Jenny remained nervously quiet as she put a few more items away. Eventually she asked in a tone she tried to keep casual, "So...are you okay with it then? Me finding Elanor?"

"I guess," Greg said shrugging. "Just please make sure it doesn't interfere with the restoration. We only have six weeks until school starts, and I'm going away in a few weeks for Ray's bachelor party, so we have to make the most of this time we have."

Jenny exhaled with relief. "It won't interfere," she said, "I promise."

Finding Elanor proved to be a bigger challenge than Jenny had thought. She spent three evenings in a row sorting through articles, biographies, and the *Choices* magazine website, unable to find anything at all suggesting where Elanor might be living now. The notion made sense, really. What successful person would want their address to be public knowledge? That would be like inviting burglars to come in. She knew what she wanted to do, but she also knew it wouldn't be well received by Greg. However, by the end of night three, Jenny didn't know what else to do.

She approached Greg, who was in the family room looking up electricians on his laptop and jotting down their contact information. "Hey, honey," she said, plopping down on the couch next to him. "I'm not having a whole lot of luck finding Elanor."

Greg didn't look up from his computer. "I'm sorry to hear that."

"Well," she proclaimed, "I'm not giving up yet. I just think I might need a little help."

"You want me to help you?"

"Not exactly," she said. "I'm not sure you'd have any more luck than I'm having. I don't think her current address is public knowledge." Jenny waited for a response from Greg that never came. He simply glanced at her skeptically, as if he knew he wasn't going to like what she was about to say next. Jenny took a deep breath and announced, "I'd like to hire a private investigator to find her."

"How much would one of those cost?"

"That's just it," Jenny said. "A lot. I think they charge by the hour, and I'm reading online that it's probably between two-fifty and three-hundred an hour."

"An *hour?*" Greg asked in disbelief. Jenny only nodded. "No," Greg said, shaking his head, "I'm fine with this being your hobby or whatever, but we can't afford to go spending money we don't have on this."

Jenny hung her head. "But it means a lot to me. This can be my early birthday present this year."

"I'm sorry," Greg said, putting his hand on Jenny's leg, "but it's just too much." Feeling satisfied that the conversation was over, Greg went back to his laptop.

Jenny obediently got off the couch and headed upstairs, blinking away tears. She collapsed on the bed and hugged her pillow, wishing Greg would understand how much she wanted to pursue this. Anger simmered under her skin, popping like bubbles. Closing her eyes and breathing deeply in an effort to get past the feeling, she focused on the sound of her breath, clearing her head of all thought. Eventually the anger began to subside, and peace took over.

"Good day, ma'am."

Jenny opened her eyes and looked around the empty room. Unlike her last encounters with the voice, she didn't feel afraid; she felt validated. "You *are* trying to tell me something," she whispered, although she wasn't sure to whom she was speaking.

She sat up slowly, weighing the options facing her. She either needed to defy her husband or ignore this voice that was reaching out for her. Greg only wanted to save money; she was sure the voice had a much larger concern. She threw her hands in the air and announced, "I have to do this."

Jenny rose and tiptoed down the stairs, retrieving her laptop. She winced as the stairs creaked while she headed back up. "Stupid old house." However, Greg didn't question what she was doing, and she hopped safely back on the bed. Feeling a bit surreal, she jotted down the names of a few private investigators to call in the morning, slid the paper into her nightstand, and closed the laptop. Satisfied with herself, she washed up, got into her pajamas, and climbed excitedly back into bed, feeling more invigorated than she had in a long time.

The next day Jenny felt like she was having an out of body experience as she set her devious plan into motion. "I'd like to pick up some paint swatches today," she mentioned casually as Greg worked intently on a list at the kitchen table. "I think we should try to get an idea of what color schemes we'd like in each room before we buy any plumbing or electrical fixtures. I might even head to the library and check out a book on homes from this era. I'd like to see what this house may have looked like originally."

"That sounds like a good idea," Greg mentioned. "While you're gone I'll do some more shopping around for plumbers. I've got an electrician coming out Wednesday at 3:00 to help us come up with a plan. We can discuss where we'd like outlets, what type of lighting we want, and stuff like that."

"Wednesday..."Jenny said thoughtfully. "What day is today?"

"Monday," Greg said in a joking tone, implying that is something Jenny should have known.

Jenny laughed. "It's always so hard to know what day it is in the summer." She tapped her forehead. "Now it's in my mental appointment book. Well, I guess I'll head out then for a little while."

"Okay, see you later," Greg muttered half-heartedly. He was already looking up the next phone number on his list.

Jenny gave him a kiss on the top of the head and scooted out the door. She drove quickly to the paint store, hurriedly gathering any tan colored swatches she could grab. She ran back out to her car and headed to the office of the private investigator she had contacted that morning.

She walked in to the simple office, which had a small waiting area and a secretary. "Hi," she said to the woman behind the desk, "I'm Jenny Watkins. Mr. Buchanan told me to drop by today to talk about a job I'd like him to do."

"Okay," the secretary said, "have a seat and I'll tell him you're here." Jenny sat in one of the three chairs in the waiting room. The secretary poked her head through an open door, announced Jenny's presence, and then said to Jenny, "Go ahead in. He's expecting you."

Jenny thanked the secretary as she walked past and went into the unkempt office. Mr. Buchanan was a middle-aged man in a disheveled suit sitting behind a desk piled with papers. She wasn't quite sure how this man would be able to find anything, let alone a woman's address, but she figured she had nothing to lose. Except three hundred dollars. And perhaps a peaceful existence at home.

He stood up and outstretched his hand, "Kyle Buchanan."

Jenny shook his hand. "Jenny Watkins."

"Pleasure, Ms. Watkins. Please have a seat." Jenny sat down in front of his desk. "So tell me what brings you in here today."

"Well," Jenny said, "My husband and I just purchased a house…a 1933 colonial in need of a lot of work. I wanted to find the original owners so I could ask what the house used to look like…you know, so we could make it look similar when we renovate."

"I see," Mr. Buchanan said.

"Well, through real estate records I was able to find out that Elanor Whitby lived there when she was a child. Elanor Whitby is the founder of *Choices* magazine. However, the one thing I can't find out is where she is now. That's where you come in."

"You'd like me to find her for you."

"Yes, sir." Jenny swallowed nervously, convinced that this private investigator was going to question her real motives any second.

"Well," he said, "before I take the job you need to be aware of some safety precautions. First, I'll need to do a background check on you before I find anyone for you. I need to make sure you're not

19

wanted by the police, or you don't have a bunch of restraining orders on you or anything."

"Understandable."

"Next," he continued, "you need to understand that some people don't want to be found. I'll need to talk with this...Ms. Whitby, is it?"

"Yes, sir."

"I'll need to talk with Ms. Whitby and make sure she's okay with meeting you. I won't disclose anybody's location unless they give me the okay. I don't want to be responsible for making anybody's life unpleasant."

"Also understandable." Jenny nodded approvingly. She felt relieved that Mr. Buchanan had apparently bought her story about the renovation and was willing to take the case.

"Then there's the matter of money." Mr. Buchanan was speaking as if reading off cue cards. "I charge three hundred dollars per hour, and I do charge even if the person says they don't want to be found. You're paying for my time, not results."

"How long do you think it will take to find her?" Jenny asked nervously.

"Honestly, not that long. If she's not purposely in hiding for any reason, I can probably find her in less than an hour's time. It doesn't sound like she's necessarily hiding from anyone."

Jenny shook her head. "No, probably not." She thought about the money, and how upset Greg would be if he knew what she was doing. "Can I make a strange arrangement with you?"

"Maybe," Mr. Buchanan smiled. "Depends on what it is."

"Money is a little tight for me....can you work for an hour and then stop? Even if you haven't found her?"

"I can do that," he said. "I'll just write that clause into the contract."

"Can I ask you another favor? This is actually a surprise for my husband...I thought it would be fun if I could show him pictures, maybe, of what the house used to look like." The lies flowed out of her mouth like she'd been doing it her whole life. "Could we possibly keep this arrangement between the two of us?"

"Ma'am," he said, "the vast majority of my cases involve secrecy. If I didn't know how to be discreet, I'd be out of work."

Relieved, Jenny smiled and exhaled. They spent the next couple of minutes signing the contract, and then Jenny scooted out the door. She headed quickly to the library, checking out the first book on older homes she could find, and ran back home.

Greg seemed unsuspecting when she arrived. "Did you have any luck?"

Feeling transparent again, she tried to act natural. "Kind of," she said. "I'm so indecisive when it comes to paint color. I'm sure most of these shades look the same, but I spent forever trying to decide which ones I liked best. I ended up bringing them all home."

"That's okay," he said, "better too many than not enough."

She smiled. "That's what I figured."

The next day Jenny's cell phone rang while she was in the grocery store; it was a number she didn't recognize. Optimistically, she said, "Hello?"

"Ms. Watkins?" asked a male voice on the other end.

"Yes."

"Kyle Buchanan here. I've got some good news for you. I was able to find Elanor for you, and as I suspected it wasn't that difficult. If you come by my office with three hundred dollars, I'll tell you where you can find her."

"Great," Jenny said, "I'll be there as soon as I can." She hurriedly filled her grocery cart and checked out. Before too long the groceries were loaded into her car, and she was on her way to the ATM machine.

"Greg's going to kill me," she sang under her breath as she punched in her ATM code. "Greg's going to kill me. Greg's going to kill me." The machine spit out fifteen twenty dollar bills, and she quickly got in her car and headed to Kyle Buchanan's office.

Jenny handed the money over to Kyle, who said, "Ms. Whitby is living in a nursing home about forty minutes from here in Lumberton. The name of the place is Maple Estates. I have the address here for you." He handed Jenny a piece of paper. "She seemed eager to meet you. She said she doesn't get a lot of visitors these days, and she's excited to tell you about the old place. It seems she still has her wits about her, luckily for you."

Jenny smiled, eager to excuse herself and get home before Greg got suspicious. "That's great. Thank you so much."

21

"My pleasure," Kyle said. "I wish all of my cases were this easy. And pleasant."

Jenny imagined he found himself in the middle of more messy divorces than anyone ought to be, and she surmised he meant what he said. With a handshake she left his office and ran out to her car, trying to formulate an excuse as to why a routine grocery store trip took so long.

Greg did indeed ask why she was gone so long, and Jenny muttered the explanation she'd come up with on the way home. Being new to the area had its advantages. "Promise you won't laugh?" she said. "I got lost on the way home." She stuck out her lip. "I think the ice cream is melted."

He let out a snort. "Why didn't you just use your GPS? You have it on your phone…"

"I know," she said, "but I wanted to get home by intuition. Sometimes the best way to learn a new area is to get lost in it."

Jenny felt somewhat guilty as she unloaded the groceries. She hated lying to him, feeling strangely unfaithful, but she also felt that he'd given her no choice. Had he been supportive, she wouldn't have had to be so secretive. In an ideal world, she could be sharing her excitement with him.

She decided she'd visit Elanor the next day, and then be honest with Greg about where she was when she returned. She was hoping to come back with some show-stopping news that would bring him on board, making him more understanding of why she'd felt the need to pursue this in the first place. With any luck, by the following evening, Greg would be just as excited about this as she was.

Chapter 4

March, 1964

Unable to sleep, Elanor crept out onto the deck of her house that overlooked Lake Wimsat. The night was unseasonably warm, and the gentle breeze felt invigorating. The lake always gave her an inexplicable sense of serenity, even at her darkest moments. She reflected back to a time seven years earlier when this lake had been witness to the heartbreak of a kind, love struck young boy. She wondered where Ronald was now, hoping he was happy. She didn't regret her relationship with him, nor did she regret ending it. However, she did regret the *way* she ended it. She should have had the courage to break up with him sooner. She still suffered pangs of guilt about that, but no amount of guilt could change the past. The best she could do was make sure she never repeated the same mistake in the future.

She glanced over her shoulder into her bedroom window, wherein lay a wonderful, unsuspecting man who didn't realize his world was going to be turned upside down in the morning. Although Mike and Ronald had very little in common, the end result was going to be the same…heartbreak at the hands of a woman who, by her own admission, may have been born without a soul.

Mike was everything that Ronald had not been. He was fiercely independent, supportive, and a progressive thinker. He reveled in Elanor's accomplishments, undaunted by the notion of being with a woman more successful than he was. On paper, Mike had all of the characteristics of a man Elanor should have been willing to marry, but she simply couldn't bring herself to have anything more than a brotherly love for him. The absence of feeling wasn't due to lack of effort. For several years she had been going through the motions, believing that if she just played the role, eventually the romantic feelings would surface. However, she couldn't deny how she felt—or how she didn't feel—about this man who treated her like she walked on water. Somehow, even the perfect man wasn't good enough for her.

She wondered if there was something wrong with her—some sort of chemical misfire in her brain that made her unlike every other woman on the planet. At times she had thought about disregarding her feelings and pursuing a life of marriage and children anyway. That lifestyle worked for most women. Why not her? However, she always decided she couldn't betray herself like that. For whatever reason, she was programmed to march to a beat of a different drummer. She was destined to walk the earth alone. That notion was fine for her; she just needed to stop leaving a series of broken-hearted men in her wake.

She placed her elbows on the railing of the deck and rested her head in her hands. She was dreading the task the morning would bring, but she had become painfully aware of Mike's increased presence at her house. He was apparently becoming quite comfortable sleeping over, and she sensed that soon he'd be expecting the relationship to progress to a level she couldn't accommodate. Desperate to avoid another ill-fated marriage proposal, she knew she had to initiate a break up. She only hoped he hadn't already purchased a ring.

She looked down at her bare finger, wondering if this was going to be a decision she would ultimately regret. She placed her hand on her belly which, because of her own doing, would never bear children. This lifestyle suited her now, but what about when she was older? With no siblings, no spouse, and no children, she would truly grow old alone. Would she be consumed with regret then? Would she look back at this moment, desperately wishing she could take back her decision to let an amazing man walk out of her life? Was she about to make a giant mistake?

She let out a sigh, knowing she'd already answered these questions for herself. She was just experiencing last-minute jitters. She took one last look out at the lake, admiring how beautiful it looked when illuminated by moonlight, feeling that familiar sense of calm the lake always brought her. This was indeed for the best...for everybody. Mike was a phenomenal man, deserving of a woman who was madly in love with him; if Elanor wasn't that woman, she had to let him go. By allowing fear to get the better of her, she'd be condemning Mike to a compromised life, and she cared about him too much to allow that.

She returned to her bedroom and slid under the sheets next to Mike. He didn't stir as she wrapped her arm around him and held him for the last time. Part of her would miss this—miss him—but not enough to justify living a fraudulent life. For now she would just enjoy the rhythmic sound of his breathing and cherish these last moments in the company of a man.

She knew she couldn't do this anymore. She couldn't break any more hearts. This had to be the last man she'd allow herself to become close to.

Chapter 5

2013

The following day Jenny seized the opportunity while Greg was at the hardware store to simply leave a note on the table. "Be back later," it said, with no other explanation offered. She turned off her phone to avoid the third degree, clutched the directions to Maple Estates in her hand, and headed off to Lumberton.

She was impressed by the facility as she pulled into the parking lot. Clearly this was a place where the wealthy folks spent their final days. She thought of her own future, realizing that a life like this was not in the cards for her. In a way, she felt saddened.

She got out of her car and approached the front door dizzy with excitement. She couldn't believe what she was doing. What on earth was Elanor going to say when Jenny announced she'd heard mysterious voices saying names—her name among them? The whole scenario was utterly surreal.

Jenny went through the sliding double doors and approached the desk. "I'm here to see Elanor Whitby."

The woman behind the desk smiled pleasantly and asked Jenny to sign in. "Have you been here before?"

"No, ma'am."

"I'll need a copy of your driver's license," she said.

Jenny complied. "The address isn't current; I just moved here," Jenny said, providing the woman with her new address. The receptionist made the change to the photocopy of the license. After check-in, Jenny dutifully followed the directions to Elanor's room. After many twists and turns, she was at last at the door, which stood slightly ajar. She knocked gently heard and a woman's voice say, "Come in."

Jenny nudged the door open slowly to see a frail, white-haired woman sitting upright in her adjustable bed. Elanor looked more fragile than Jenny had expected, but a twinkle in her bright blue eyes suggested that Kyle Buchanan had been right when he had said she was still cognizant. Jenny smiled apprehensively at her and asked, "Ms. Whitby?"

"Oh, call me Elanor," she said enthusiastically. "You must be the young woman who bought my old house! Come in, dear, please. And do tell me your name."

"Jenny. Jenny Watkins." She slowly walked through the door, noting the room looked more like an apartment than a nursing home. The walls were a warm honey color as opposed to a sterile white, and the colorful curtains matched the upholstery of the recliner and loveseat in the corner. She had her own kitchen area and a giant flat screen television on the far wall. Without realizing it, Jenny had frozen as she looked around the room.

"Have a seat, dear, please." Elanor gestured toward the recliner. "Actually, can you pull it over here closer? My eyes and ears aren't what they used to be."

Jenny slid the recliner over next to the bed and sat stiffly on the edge.

"So…please…tell me a little about yourself," Elanor began.

Jenny smiled politely. "Well, like I said, my name is Jenny. I'm twenty-six; I'm married, and I am a teacher."

"A teacher! How wonderful. What grade do you teach?"

"I taught second grade back in Kentucky, where we're from, but this year I got a job teaching fourth grade at Evansdale Elementary."

"That's fabulous. I have the utmost respect for anyone who can work with kids. I like kids, but only from a comfortable distance. Do you like teaching?"

"Most days," Jenny admitted. "Some days are tougher than others. I never realized how hard it would be."

"I'm sure it is hard. Y'all are an underpaid bunch, that's for sure. But I'm glad you like your job. I was fortunate enough to love mine. In fact, I loved it to the point where it didn't even feel like work."

"You ran *Choices* magazine, right?"

"Sure did! And I often put in eighty hour weeks, so it's a good thing I enjoyed it."

"Wow," Jenny marveled, "that's crazy."

"You know what else is crazy?" Elanor asked with a mischievous grin. "Buying that house you bought. I admit I haven't seen it in a while, but the last time I drove by it, it looked like a shit hole. What on earth possessed you to buy that thing?"

Jenny laughed, sinking slightly back into her chair. "My husband and I are planning to fix it up and then sell it in a few years for a profit. We're going to use that money to start a family."

"Good for you, although you've got your work cut out for you. I can't believe how bad it looks. It's a shame, too, because it was a beautiful house once upon a time."

"My husband and I were just saying that the other day."

"Do you know the story of how that house came to be?"

"No," Jenny replied, hopeful that the story would help unravel the mystery of Steve O'dell. "But I'd love to hear it."

"In order to understand how it came to be, you first have to realize that Whitby money was old money. Very old money. And there was lots of it. You know how they say some people are born with a silver spoon in their mouths? Well, my father had flatware for eight." Elanor scratched her head. "Looking back on it, it boggles my mind when I think how high-and-mighty my father used to act because he was rich, yet he hadn't done a damn thing to earn any of that money. All he did was get born to the right parents." She shook her head in disgust. After a moment she snapped back into the present and said, "Listen to me, rambling like this. If I'm not careful I'm going to turn into one of the people that wander the halls around here, wearing my underwear outside of my pants and muttering about the war and some other shit that doesn't make any sense."

Jenny bit her lip to keep from laughing.

"Anyway, my mother was a working-class girl from Evansdale, but she was a beauty. Inside and out. One summer when she was a teenager she went up to Virginia to be a nanny for her aunt and uncle, and she met my father there. Apparently he fell for her pretty hard, because when she went back to Evansdale at the end of the summer, my father followed her. Shortly after that they were married. That was 1928.

"As you probably know, the stock market crashed the following year, but my lucky bastard of a father wasn't that hard hit by it. He was a money-in-the-mattress kind of man, so he didn't have a whole lot invested in stocks. While everyone else lost their shirts, my parents were pretty much untouched.

"But my mother was horrified by what happened to the people of her town. They were good people, the people of Evansdale, and many of them didn't even know where their next meal was coming from. She begged my father to help, but he didn't believe in handouts, so he commissioned the construction of the house. It took a long time to build, and it employed a lot of people in the process. My mother even hired some of the local women to sew custom curtains and bedding. That house put food on a lot of people's tables, and my parents were beloved in the community because of it."

"That's *fascinating*," Jenny said genuinely. "I had no idea the house had such history."

"I'm sure you wondered, though, why such a big house was built right smack dab in the center of a middle class neighborhood. You have to admit, that house sticks out like a sore thumb."

"Yes, it does, actually."

"You know what's funny, though? My dad had this whole big house built with lots of bedrooms so he could fill them with boys to carry on his precious family name…and what did he have? One girl." Elanor chuckled. "I bet he was shooting blanks."

Jenny opened her mouth to say something, but only a tiny sound came out.

"You know what's even funnier?" Elanor added. "I didn't even go on to have any kids. When I die, this branch of the Whitby family tree dies with me. You know what that is? That's karma, kicking my dad in the ass. I'm not really religious or anything, but I can't help but think this is somebody's way of telling my dad to shut the hell up and quit bragging about shit he didn't earn."

For a moment Jenny questioned if she was in a nursing home or a truck stop, but she was amused nonetheless. In her house growing up, only the boys were allowed to speak with such indiscretion. To hear it from a woman—and an elderly woman at that—was humorous indeed.

"But I guess a lesson on my family history isn't what you're here for, now is it?" Elanor continued, "I imagine you'd like to hear about what the house used to look like."

Jenny leaned forward in her chair again. "Well," she began uncomfortably, "there's actually another reason why I'm here."

"Oh? What is that, dear?"

Jenny let out a sigh, unsure of how to proceed. "I'm wondering if the name Steve O'dell means anything to you."

Elanor froze. "Did you say Steve O'dell?"

"Yes ma'am."

"Do you know him? Did he send you here?" Elanor asked eagerly.

"Well, no." Jenny shook her head, sighing again, painfully aware of the ridiculousness of her next words. "Ever since I moved into that house, I've heard a voice. The first two times it said Steve O'dell, and then the third time it said your name."

Elanor seemed shocked. "A *voice* said my name? And Steve's?"

"I know it sounds strange, but yes." Jenny winced, preparing to hear that she was out of line and needed to leave. However, those words never came, so after a short while she delicately continued. "I assume from your reaction that you know him."

"I did." Elanor seemed distant as she spoke. "A long time ago."

Did. That word didn't get lost on Jenny, who became suddenly aware that she may have brought up a touchy subject. Unsure of what to say next, Jenny sat silent, allowing Elanor to continue at her own pace.

"He was my boyfriend back when I was young. We were desperately in love, or so I thought. One weekend I went away, and when I came back he was gone. He'd apparently left town without saying goodbye or anything." Elanor lowered her eyes, her pain still evident after all these years.

"Did you ever see him again?"

"No," Elanor said sadly. "It's as if he vanished into thin air."

Things began to click, albeit slightly, inside Jenny's brain. There *was* something she was supposed to be figuring out. Suddenly she felt markedly less foolish for being there.

"I did hear one other message that may mean something to you, if you'd care to hear it."

Elanor snapped to attention. "Oh, yes, please."

"I heard *good day, ma'am.*"

Elanor raised her hand to cover her mouth as tears welled in her eyes. "That was our code," she said weakly. "I'd almost forgotten…"

Aware of the gravity of the situation, Jenny reduced her voice to a whisper. "Code for what?"

"I love you," Elanor said, staring off into space. "We kept our relationship a secret because we knew my parents wouldn't approve. The way he told me he loved me in public was to nod his head at me and say *good day, ma'am.* I would reply with *good day* as well, and that was my way of saying I loved him too."

Jenny had a million questions, but she knew she couldn't bombard Elanor with too much at once. Elanor looked frail enough as it was; Jenny certainly didn't want to upset her any more than she already had.

After a while Elanor looked optimistically at Jenny. "Did the voice say anything else?"

"No, ma'am. But that's why I'm here. I feel like I'm supposed to be figuring something out, and I was hoping you could help me do it."

"I would love to figure out what happened to Steve. I've led a full life—I really have—but as I lie here in this bed, my one regret is that I'll never know for sure what happened that weekend. Or why. If I could get answers to those questions, I feel like I'll be able to die peacefully."

"Well, maybe we can find some answers," Jenny replied, cheerfully patting Elanor's bed rail. "And hopefully we'll have a good, long time to do it."

"Oh, honey, I appreciate your optimism, but I'm quite sure I don't have too much time left." Elanor spoke without an ounce of self-pity in her voice. "I was diagnosed with cancer a while ago. I decided to skip the chemo and radiation and all of that other life-lengthening crap. I've sold my business. I'm nobody's grandma." She held out her hands, gesturing to her room. "This is all I have now, and I didn't really feel like it was worth prolonging, you know? Besides, chemo makes you feel like shit. The only thing worse than sitting in this bed all day would be sitting in this bed feeling like shit."

Despite the chipper nature of Elanor's tone, Jenny felt sympathy for the stranger in front of her. Eager to change the subject, Jenny proclaimed, "Well, then, why don't you tell me a little bit about Steve O'dell, and we'll see if we can figure this out for you?"

"Gosh," Elanor sighed, dredging up memories she clearly hadn't recalled in decades. "Where to begin? Steve was unlike any other man I'd ever met. He truly was. He was a drifter who essentially figured out his next destination by throwing a dart at a map. He ended up in Evansdale because that's where the guy he hitched a ride with was going." Elanor patted Jenny's hand. "Now keep in mind, in the 1950s hitchhiking was a perfectly acceptable means of transportation."

"Understood," Jenny said smiling.

Elanor went back to her memories, looking somber. "Poor kid. He'd had a horrible upbringing. His dad was an alcoholic who used to beat up his mother and the kids. Steve was the youngest in his family, and he was much too eager to get out of that house to wait until he turned 18. He dropped out of school and hit the road at about fifteen, never looking back." Elanor shook her head. "It's a shame, too, because he was smart as a whip. If he'd have born into a family like mine, he could have been the damn president. Instead he found himself traveling from town to town, taking odd jobs to get by. Fortunately for him he was so smart, because he was able to pick up various trades quite quickly.

"But he never stayed in any one place too long. According to him, no place he visited ever quite scratched the itch like he would have wanted. No place ever felt like home. Having no obligations, he was able to pack up his meager belongings and move to the next town quite easily. Fortunately for me, one of those towns ended up being Evansdale."

"So how did you meet?" Jenny asked.

"Steve showed up at our door one day when I was a teenager, out of the blue, looking for work. Our house was the obvious choice, being the most beautiful in the area. Remember, my father was okay with the idea of helping people, but he wasn't one for handouts, so he offered Steve a job for a month. Steve was tasked with doing yard work, repairs around the house...stuff like that. If Steve proved himself to be a good worker in that first month, he could stay on board. Of course, Steve had an amazing work ethic, so he passed the test with flying colors. He stayed on as our jack-of-all-trades guy, and my father paid him enough for him to afford a room in a nearby house and get by.

"Although, looking back, I'm not really sure how much my father did pay him. The room he rented was just that…a room. It had its own separate entrance, so it was private, and it had a bathroom, but that was it. It didn't have a kitchen or anything; Steve used to heat up his dinners in a pot over a camping stove. It wasn't much of a life for a man who worked so hard."

"But you guys ended up falling in love?"

"After a while, yes. At first I didn't think too much of Steve. He was quite a bit older than me…he was probably 25 or 26 when he showed up at our door. He wasn't incredibly good looking, either. I had no real reason to notice him. But my parents had always raised me to be polite, so I would bring him lemonade or watermelon when he was working outside on those hot days. It gets hot here in Evansdale in the summer."

"I've noticed," Jenny added.

"I'm sure you have," Elanor laughed. "Anyway, there I was, a typical teenager, looking for constant entertainment. If nothing else was going on I'd stay outside and chat with Steve as he did his work. It didn't take too long before he started to fascinate me. Keep in mind I was a very sheltered girl who had never left Evansdale. Here was this well-traveled guy who had seen so much—done so much. The stories that man could tell were mindboggling to me, and he was just talking about his everyday life.

"Hearing him tell his stories changed the way I thought about the world. It occurred to me that he had worked so hard for everything he owned—which was very little. I, on the other hand, hadn't worked a day in my life, yet I lived in a huge house and had the fanciest of things. It didn't seem right. He should have had the big house. He should have had the best of everything. I should have been the one heating up my dinner on a camping stove." Elanor shook her head in disgust. "It's just not right."

Jenny leaned back in the recliner and crossed her legs. "So how did you guys round that corner from a work relationship to love?

I imagine it must have taken a pretty bold move on his part to hit on the boss's daughter."

"It would have been a bold move if he was the one that did it," Elanor said bluntly. "I'm actually the one who made the first move."

"Oh really?" Jenny had to smile.

"If I'd waited for him to do it, I'd probably still be waiting. I swear I flirted as much as humanly possible, and I could tell by the way he looked at me that he was smitten, but he never did take that leap. I guess there was that whole *I could lose my job and my livelihood* thing to worry about." Elanor playfully rolled her eyes. "I didn't really have anything at stake."

"So how did you do it?" Jenny asked eagerly.

"Well, it was a day when he was doing some inside work. An upstairs pipe had leaked and messed up the ceiling downstairs, and Steve was fixing the ceiling. My parents were out for the afternoon, so I hung around him while he worked. Normally we talked about his adventures, or politics, or how horrible segregation was, but this day I asked him point blank about women. I asked if he ever had a girlfriend, and he said he never stayed in one place long enough to get one. At that point I figured he'd be receptive, so I walked over to him and just planted a kiss on him. And boy, did he ever kiss me back." Elanor looked distant for a moment and smiled, clearly reliving the moment. Snapping back into reality, she looked at Jenny and said, "That's when he confessed that I was the reason he'd stayed in Evansdale as long as he did. He said he'd never felt about a woman the way he'd felt about me. He said I scratched that itch he'd had his whole life." Elanor smiled, but then she looked down at her lap and the smile faded.

"So you guys became a couple?"

"In secret, yes. My parents would have been furious if they knew, so we didn't tell a soul. Not any of my friends…not anybody. We devised that *good day, ma'am* code so we could express our love freely in public. But other than that we were extremely careful. We knew it could have been disastrous if anyone found out.

"As a result, I became an expert at lying," Elanor proclaimed. "I don't know how many times I told my parents I was going out with my friends when I actually went over to Steve's place. My parents had a pretty active social life, too, so there were plenty of times I was home alone and Steve came over. If ever they came home earlier than expected, it wasn't any big deal to see Steve there. They just figured he was doing some extra work, and they liked that. Once my dad even gave him a tip for working extra hours. How's that for a little irony? My dad paid a guy to come over and fool around with his daughter." Elanor thought for a moment. "Does that make me a prostitute?" After more deliberation she added, "No, it doesn't work that way."

Jenny laughed out loud, almost forgetting Elanor was sixty years her senior. "How long did you manage to keep the relationship a secret?"

"For about a year, I think. It actually wasn't that hard to keep it from my parents," Elanor continued. "They didn't suspect anything because they never imagined in a million years that I'd be attracted to Steve. I was a blond-haired, blue-eyed, extremely wealthy teenager, and Steve was an average looking handyman in his mid-twenties. On paper we had no reason to be a couple. But he was the most amazing person I'd ever met."

"What made him so amazing?" Jenny asked with a smile.

"Oh, goodness. So many things," Elanor replied. After giving the subject a little thought, she finally said, "He was just so grateful. For a man who had so little, he was surely appreciative. I guess his value system was different than most people. He didn't get much happiness out of material things—what he valued was his freedom. He had the ability to go anywhere or do anything. Through his travels, he saw so many people dredging through life as if it was pre-programmed. You grow up, get married, the man works, the woman doesn't, you have kids, you retire, you die. A lot of those people weren't happy, even though society had deemed them a success. Steve, on the other hand, was a failure from a societal standpoint, but he had traveled the country. He did work he enjoyed. If he stopped enjoying it, he'd move somewhere else and get a job doing something different." A smile appeared on her face. "He was *happy*."

Jenny looked shamefully at her lap.

"But I was also attracted to his progressive attitude," Elanor added. "I know it doesn't seem like a big deal now, but Steve felt very strongly that people shouldn't be judged by the color of their skin. Keep in mind that back then there were separate restaurants, separate water fountains, separate schools…It was amazing how differently people got treated based solely on what they looked like. But Steve knew better. He had the wherewithal to get to know someone before drawing any conclusions about them. He liked—and disliked—people of every race, but he based that decision entirely on character."

"He seems like a really great guy," Jenny concluded.

"He was." Elanor let out a snort. "And we were going to change the world, him and me."

"Oh really?" Jenny asked. "How so?"

"We were going to get the message out. We were going to crusade for equality and advocate for free will." Elanor raised her finger in the air like a superhero. After a quick laugh she lowered her hand, adding in a more serious tone, "With his street smarts and my money and connections, we figured we had a decent shot at having a real impact." She lowered her eyes. Reducing her voice to a barely-audible whisper, she concluded, "I guess it wasn't meant to be."

Jenny responded almost as quietly as Elanor. "So what ended up happening?"

"My father caught us. He wasn't supposed to come home until after dinner one night, but he came home early because he didn't feel well. Steve and I were in my bedroom, and we didn't hear him come in." Elanor shook her head. "He caught us together. It was an ugly, ugly scene. I don't think I'd ever seen my father so angry. He fired Steve on the spot and forbade me from ever seeing him again.

"I begged my father to understand. My father had always raved about what a good worker Steve was; in fact, my father had adored him until he found out about us. I reminded him of all the wonderful things he had said about Steve, and assured him they were all true. Steve was a good, honest, hard-working man. I tried to get my father to see that he should have been pleased with my choice, but he wouldn't listen. Steve was a manual laborer. A drifter. He was poor. There was no way my father was going to allow me to be with any man who wasn't from our social circle. My father wanted me to be with a rich boy. Period. Money and social status were apparently more important than character to my father.

"I was beside myself when Steve got fired, but you have to realize my father's stubborn streak ran in the family. As stubborn as he was, I was more so. Steve got a job with a local house builder, and we continued to secretly see each other despite my father's wishes. Steve obviously didn't come to my house anymore, but I did go visit him. It may seem strange, but I was so much happier in that shitty little room Steve rented than I was in my big, beautiful house. Steve's place felt like home. Whenever I was with Steve, it felt like home." She raised her bright blue eyes to Jenny. "That's how I knew it was love."

Jenny smiled in return.

"Anyway," Elanor went on, "we continued to see each other that way for quite some time. Then, when I was twenty, my mother and I went up to Lynchburg, Virginia for a weekend for my cousin's bridal shower. When I came back, Steve was nowhere to be found. I went to his room, but it was completely empty. Everything—gone. I was stunned. I knew where his latest construction site had been, so I went there, asking the guys on the crew if they'd seen him. The foreman told me that Steve had come by and announced he was leaving town. He was in such a hurry to leave that he didn't even want his last paycheck."

"Oh my God," Jenny replied.

"I didn't get it. He had shown no indication of wanting to leave. Nothing seemed unusual between us before I left. We were just as happy as ever. That's when it hit me…maybe he didn't *decide* to leave…maybe my father found out about us and forced him to."

"You mean paid him off?" Jenny asked.

"I don't think so; Steve didn't care enough about money for that. But I think my father must have dug up some dirt on him. My dad had connections—lots of them—and I think he was able discover something Steve had done along the way that would get him in trouble. Big trouble. I think he blackmailed Steve into leaving while I was away. I can't imagine any other reason Steve would have left." Elanor shook her head and looked back at her lap. "I never forgave my father for that."

Jenny asked delicately, "And that was the last time you ever saw Steve?"

"Yes," Elanor confessed. "I waited for him, though. For a long time. I put my romantic life on hold, just sure that Steve would come back. I didn't think anyone could walk away from a love like that and not return. But maybe I was just a fool. A young, love-struck fool." Elanor glanced at Jenny. "I've come to learn in my old age that leopards don't change their spots. I realize in hindsight that I fell in love with a drifter and then felt devastated when he left town. But that's what drifters do. In a way, my heartbreak was my own fault." She looked down at her lap again. "Although, he did make promises. I don't blame myself entirely for the heartbreak. He shouldn't have made promises he wouldn't honor."

"So what happened after he left?" Jenny asked.

"Oh, lots." Elanor said, regaining her composure. "I was so mad at my father that I moved out immediately. I moved into Steve's old room, as a matter of fact. He had paid for it in advance, so the landlord let me stay there in his place for a couple of months until I had enough of my own money to start paying for it myself. I left with only the shirt on my back, so I went out and got a cashiering job. I also babysat as often as I could. I had nothing to my name, but I was bound and determined to make it on my own. I didn't want any of my father's money. That money was dirty, as far as I was concerned. It was the reason I couldn't be with Steve."

Elanor let out a laugh. "I think I went an entire month eating nothing but peanut butter sandwiches. I had one outfit that I washed in the sink. I went from being rich as hell to being as poor as anybody could be. But I was angry, and that anger fueled me. I never, not once, considered moving back into my father's house. I would have preferred to starve than live under that roof."

"What about your mother?" Jenny asked. "Did you still have a relationship with her?"

"Yes, but it was strained. I refused to be anywhere my father was, so if she wanted to spend time with me, she had to come to my place. Oh, she begged me to come home, but there was no way I would have agreed to that. No way in hell."

Elanor smiled genuinely, her blue eyes shining. "But you know what happened? I worked every possible minute I could, and I was able to buy myself some silverware, and a plate, and a pot, and eventually my own camping stove, thank you very much. I bought some new clothes. And you know, I had never been prouder in my life. Granted, I was wearing clothes from the clearance rack and second-hand stores, but they were *my* clothes. That plate I was eating on? It was *my* plate. I bought it with my own money that I earned myself. Nobody gave it to me. It was rightfully mine. And it was the best feeling in the world.

"In a strange kind of way, being penniless was the best thing that ever could have happened to me. I learned the value of a dollar and the satisfaction of a hard day's work. My whole life prior to that, my responsibilities were just to look pretty and be gracious. And be a

Whitby. If I did those things, I got everything handed to me for free. I'm so glad I didn't continue to be that person. I hate that person.

"Anyway, I still had the desire to change the world, even if Steve wasn't around to do it with me. I was actually doubly inspired because of my anger toward my father. I wanted to let people know that they didn't have to do what was expected of them. Sometimes, in order to be true to yourself, you have to piss some people off. And you have to *write* some people off. And you have to step on some toes. And sometimes, you have to take some giant steps backward to go forward. Every once in a while you need to go back and make that right turn you missed somewhere along the line. It's what I had just done, and it was the best thing that had ever happened to me. I wanted other people to know that so they wouldn't stay on the straight path simply out of fear. Fear is not a reason."

Jenny once again looked at her lap.

"I had to get the message out—it was bursting inside of me— so I eventually bought myself a second-hand typewriter and made up a pamphlet." Elanor explained. "I stood in front of a store and handed it out to women on the street. The women looked at me like I was crazy, but they took it. The following week I had drafted another pamphlet and passed it out again. The women recognized me from the last time, and were, for the most part, eager to read another one. The following week I created a third, and I made up even more of them. They all got snatched up pretty quickly.

"Soon the owner of the store asked what I was doing out there. I thought he was going to ask me to leave, but instead he offered me some money to put an ad in the pamphlet. I agreed, and suddenly I was making a profit." Elanor smiled, her eyes full of pride. "That was the beginning of *Choices* magazine."

"That's fantastic," Jenny said. "It's so wonderful that you took such a devastating blow and turned it into something positive."

"It was a blessing in disguise, that whole mess. I always tell that to people; sometimes an event that seems terrible at the time turns out to be the kick in the ass you need to get going in the right direction. Although," she said sadly, "I do often think about Steve. I wonder what could have been if my father didn't interfere."

"Well, hopefully we can figure that out. I'll tell you what, Miss Elanor. I'll call a medium out to the house to do a reading. Perhaps a psychic could get a feel for what is going on in that house.

Maybe we can get an answer to whatever became of Steve, or at least find out what message someone's trying to send."

"That would be great," Elanor said gratefully. "Thank you so much. I'll pay any expenses you incur."

"Oh, that's not necessary," Jenny said.

"Please," Elanor said, "It's the least I can do. Besides, you're a teacher, so I know you don't make much. But I've got more money than I know what to do with. Shit, I don't need money in here, and I can't take it with me, right?"

"I suppose not. Well, thank you, Miss Elanor. I guess I'll just let you know how much it is, then. Honestly, I have no idea how much a medium would charge to do a reading on a house…or whatever you'd call it." The words sounded absurd coming out of Jenny's mouth.

"I'm not sure either, but whatever it takes is fine. Answers would mean more to me than any amount of money at this point."

After exchanging pleasantries, Jenny left Elanor's room, her head spinning from everything she had discovered. During the ride home, she replayed the story in her head over and over again, trying to sort it all out. One thing she did know for sure; Greg would be unable to deny that she was on to something. He'd have to forgive her spending three hundred dollars on the private investigator, and hopefully she wouldn't have to be so secretive about hiring the mediums, especially considering she would be reimbursed. She didn't see how Greg could possibly be upset.

Jenny did keep her phone off for the drive home, though, postponing the inevitable inquisition she would get from Greg. She felt bad, hoping that Greg wasn't too worried, but believing the in-person explanation she was about to give would exonerate her from any perceived wrongdoing.

She arrived home to find Greg sitting at the kitchen table with his arms folded across his chest. As soon as she walked in, he said in an irritated tone, "Did you forget something?"

Surprised by the question, Jenny racked her brain to try to figure out what he meant. Then it hit her. "Oh…It's Wednesday." She glanced at her watch, which read 4:30. She put her hand on her forehead. "We had an appointment with the electrician at 3:00."

"Correction," Greg said stubbornly, "*I* had an appointment with an electrician. *You* were nowhere to be found."

Jenny's optimism for forgiveness instantly disappeared, replaced by the familiar feeling of simmering bubbles of anger popping beneath her skin. She paused for a moment, gathering herself, trying to respond in a way that wouldn't spark an argument. She took a deep breath and said, "So what did you and the electrician come up with?"

"I don't know." Greg shrugged his shoulders. "I forgot."

Jenny closed her eyes, nearly overcome with repugnance.

"So where were you?" Greg asked bitterly. "Out hiring a private investigator?"

Elanor's words echoed in Jenny's head. *Sometimes, in order to be true to yourself, you have to piss some people off.* She straightened her posture, flipped her hair back, and said, "No, I was not out hiring a private investigator. I did that two days ago. Today I was out visiting Elanor Whitby."

Greg shook his head and gritted his teeth. "I don't know what's gotten into you. I really don't. We had a plan to come out here and fix up this house so one day we could start a family...now it seems you don't care about any of it. You're more concerned with...this *voice* you're hearing." He sighed impatiently. "I just don't get it."

"I'm not more concerned with the voice," Jenny said defensively. "But I am curious about it, and it wouldn't hurt you to be a little more supportive."

"I *was* supportive," Greg said. "Didn't I say you could look for her all you want? I just asked you not to spend money on it, but you did. I saw the bank withdrawal, Jenny. Don't even try to deny it. I also asked you to be here for an appointment with the electrician, but you weren't." He impatiently put his hands on his hips. "The way I see it, *you're* the one who's not being supportive."

"I'm done here," Jenny said, spinning on her heels and walking away. She went upstairs into her bedroom, locking the door behind her. She took several deep breaths to calm herself, but the animosity remained. She ran her trembling fingers through her hair and paced the room.

Out of the corner of her eye she noticed the laptop sitting on the nightstand from Greg's late-night price comparisons the evening before. "Bingo," she whispered. Determined to give Elanor some answers, Jenny opened the laptop and researched some psychics and mediums in the area. The list was much longer than she had imagined. With so many options, she was unsure of which one to choose, or even a good method of narrowing them down. They all claimed to be real. They all had testimonials from satisfied customers. However, Jenny knew that true psychic ability didn't grow on trees, and most—if not all—of these characters would prove to be phony. Undeterred, she chose a name of one who looked promising and pulled her phone out of her pocket.

Sometimes, you have to step on some toes.

Chapter 6

The following day Miss Belle arrived at the house at 3:00. Greg was home but had spent the entire day avoiding Jenny, and that trend only continued after the psychic's arrival. Jenny alone went out to greet Miss Belle but had an uneasy feeling as the woman emerged from her car. They shook hands, and Jenny had the distinct impression she was shaking the hand of a professional fraud.

To test the woman's true ability, Jenny didn't give any details of what she knew or had heard. She simply said she wanted a reading of the house since it was old and she was just curious if it had any spirits roaming around in it.

Jenny invited the psychic in, and Miss Belle immediately closed her eyes. "Yes," she said, "I'm definitely getting something." She allowed herself in and wandered the house aimlessly for a while. She didn't say a word, but acted as if she were using all five senses to receive messages. After a short time she said to Jenny, "There is a presence here, but don't worry, it's a friendly one. It's a child. May I go upstairs?"

"Of course," Jenny said politely, even though she was fully aware this was just a waste of time.

Miss Belle headed up the stairs, wandering in and out of each room, including the one where Greg was installing a ceiling fan. He looked up and watched her skeptically for a moment, then went back to his work, shaking his head.

Miss Belle stopped in one of the smaller bedrooms. "Yes," she said, "This was the child's room. I feel sickness in here. Pneumonia."

Jenny feigned interest, "So a child died of pneumonia in here?"

"Yes," Miss Belle said pensively. "A little girl. About eight or nine, I'm guessing. She's still here, wanting to play. She may not realize she's passed."

Jenny frowned, "That's *fascinating.*" Miss Belle had no idea she was being made fun of.

"You may notice some odd happenings from time to time," Miss Belle explained. "Lights on when you swear you've turned them off. Inexplicable noises. Items not where you've left them…that kind of thing. But don't be alarmed; she's just playing."

"So she's a prankster." Jenny couldn't help herself.

"Most of them are," Miss Belle added. "The children, that is. The older ones can sometimes be trouble."

Jenny nodded, eager to get this so-called reading over with so she could go back to stripping wallpaper. After a few pleasantries, and a check for two hundred and fifty dollars, Miss Belle left.

Feeling a strong desire to end the standoff with her husband, Jenny went up to where Greg was working and leaned in the doorway. "Boy, she was a nut case," Jenny said.

"And how much did that nut case cost us?" Greg asked without looking up.

"Nothing. Elanor asked me to hire a medium on her behalf. We're not paying for any of this."

That seemed to instantly relax Greg. "I wish you would have told me that sooner."

"I would have," Jenny said calmly, "but you made me too angry." She walked into the room and sat down on the floor near Greg. "Look, I'm sorry I forgot about the electrician yesterday. I really am. But I know I'm on to something here. Elanor believes that too. It turns out the man's name that I heard was her boyfriend, who disappeared one day, never to be heard from again. I want to try to get Elanor some answers, but I'm afraid she may not have that long to live; she has cancer, which she decided not to treat."

Greg sighed. "As long as we're not paying for it, I guess I'm okay with it. But please try not to let it interfere with the restoration. Our lives have to come first. Our *real* lives."

In an ideal world, Greg would have shown more interest, but Jenny was grateful for the minimal amount of support he was showing. It was better than opposition. She still didn't feel like sharing the details with him; he wouldn't have appreciated them. She decided to leave the conversation where it was, in a somewhat amicable place. "It's a deal," she said.

She got up and started to leave the room. "I told the electrician about the quadruple outlets," Greg called without looking. He took a wire splicer out of his tool box.

"What?" Jenny asked.

"The quadruple outlets. You had mentioned once that you thought the kitchen and bathrooms should have quadruple outlets. You thought it would be a nice selling point for women." Greg cut off the end of a wire. "I mentioned it to the electrician, and he thought it was a good idea."

Fully aware that was Greg's way of apologizing, Jenny smiled and continued out the door.

Jenny put a bowl of green beans on the dinner table as Greg, already seated, put some chicken on his plate. She sat down and took a sip of her water. "I was thinking I would like to hire another psychic to come to the house, but we don't have the money to pay for it. I'd like to go out to visit Elanor again tomorrow and see if she'll reimburse me for Miss Belle. Maybe she'll even give me an advance on the next one."

"That's a good idea," Greg said. "I don't want you spending any more money on this unless you know for sure she'll be good for it."

Jenny smiled inside; she wasn't surprised that Greg was okay with the idea since it involved collecting money. "Oh, she's good for it. This woman has money out the wazoo. You should see the place she's staying. It's the nicest nursing home I've ever seen."

Jenny frowned and continued. "You know, her wealth is actually making me somewhat nervous. I'm afraid she's going to think I'm only after her money. How's it going to look when I go in and say, 'hey…you don't really know me, but why don't you give me a ton of money, and I promise I'll use it to hire psychics for you.'" She stabbed at some chicken. "I wouldn't blame her for telling me to get the hell out."

"Well, why don't you print out some of the information you got from the web about some of these psychics, and then let Elanor decide which ones to hire? She can make the checks out to them, not to you, and then she'll have to know you're not using the money for yourself."

Jenny waved her fork at Greg. "See! This is why I'm with you. It's so simple, yet I never would have thought of that."

"And while you're at it," Greg said, "Why don't you bring that paperwork from that private investigator you hired and see if she'll pay you back for that, too? Three hundred dollars is a lot of money." He raised his eyebrow at her.

Jenny sighed. "I guess I'm not any good at being sneaky." She took a bite of her dinner. "You know, it'll be a weird conversation to go in and ask for that money."

"It can't be any weirder than going in and telling her you've heard voices."

Jenny twisted her face. "Touche."

The next morning, Jenny knocked gently on Elanor's half-open door. "Come in," she called, and her face lit up immediately upon seeing Jenny. "Oh, hello, dear! Do come in! I'm afraid you'll have to tell me your name again, though. I never forget a face, but I've always been terrible with names."

"Jenny. Jenny Watkins." She pulled up the same chair and sat next to the bed.

"Oh, that's right. Jenny Watkins. So what brings you here today, Jenny Watkins? Have you gotten any more messages?"

"No, I'm afraid not," she admitted, "and unfortunately the medium I hired was a fraud. I spent two hundred and fifty dollars for nothing." Jenny let out a nervous laugh. "She told me the house was haunted by a nine year old girl who died of pneumonia."

"Oh, well that's clearly not true," Elanor said bluntly. "Did you tell her she was full of shit?"

Jenny laughed. "No, I was polite."

"I wouldn't have been," Elanor noted. "I stopped being polite decades ago. Once I hit forty I started calling a spade a spade. But I guess you're not there yet." Elanor winked.

"No, not yet."

"Mark my words," Elanor said. "When you turn thirty, you'll become chronically cold. When you hit forty, you'll stop giving a shit about trying to be polite." She pointed at Jenny. "I'm telling you, it's like clockwork."

"I'll make a note of that." Trying to stick to the issue at hand, Jenny added, "I'm sorry she was a fraud, though," Jenny said, "I feel like I wasted your money."

Elanor made a dismissive gesture with her hand. "Oh, don't worry about that."

"Well," Jenny said, "I'd like to try again with another psychic, if you're willing."

"Oh, definitely. I'm willing to do whatever it takes."

"The only thing is," Jenny said delicately, "I don't really have the cash to hire another one." She looked down at her lap. "We just bought the house and all…"

"No need to explain," Elanor said laughing. "I should have thought of that before. Be a dear and hand me my purse, and I'll write you a check."

As she crossed the room to get Elanor's purse from a counter, Jenny added, "My husband had the idea that you could help me decide which psychics to hire next, and you could make checks out directly to them. That way you know I'm on the up and up."

"Well, I don't doubt that you're on the up and up," Elanor said. "You knew about our code. No one could have possibly known that." Elanor took the purse as Jenny handed it to her, "Although I do like the idea of making checks out to the psychics, just because it's easier."

Jenny let out a sigh. "There's one other thing." She paused, finding it difficult to say the next sentence. "My husband…he's a bit of a penny pincher. He's a little upset that I spent the money hiring the private investigator to find you, and he was wondering if you'd mind, um, covering that."

Elanor laughed at the difficulty Jenny had making the request. "Well, that's reasonable. Darling, don't ever feel funny asking for that. So how much was the private investigator?"

"Three hundred dollars."

"Three hundred dollars? That's quite a bit of money," Elanor said, a mischievous spark gleaming in her eye. "I would think for that kind of money he should have at least done his job naked."

Jenny laughed but then cringed at the thought of Kyle Buchanan naked. "I'm actually kind of glad he kept his clothes on, to tell you the truth."

"Oh. Too bad." Elanor added, thumbing through her checkbook. "If my math is correct, I guess I owe you five-fifty." She filled out a check and handed it to Jenny.

Jenny smiled. "Thank you, Miss Elanor. Well, I've brought some information about some psychics. Would you like to take a look?"

"Of course, dear," Elanor said, "But I'm not sure I'll be able to pick out a good one."

"Me neither," Jenny replied, "but maybe if we work together we can come up with something." Jenny and Elanor spent the next hour reading over psychic blurbs, trying to weed out the phonies. Jenny left with a list of five psychics to contact, blank checks made out to those psychics, and a personal check made out to her for five hundred and fifty dollars. She also left with a smile on her face, feeling as if the weight of the world had been lifted off her shoulders. Perhaps there was a way she could get Elanor the answers she wanted without making a mess of her marriage.

Over the next few days, Jenny had three more psychics over to the house; each one proved to be as phony as the one before. At first she was polite to them, entertaining their far-fetched prophecies and declarations. After a while, however, her patience began to wear thin. She could tell each one of them was fake the second she greeted them, and she was tired of wasting her time listening to fictitious ghost stories. Greg was clearly growing tired of it as well.

"So when are you going to give up on this?" Greg asked her as one of the so-called psychics drove away.

"As soon as I find one that's real," Jenny proclaimed.

"And what if that never happens? How many times are you going to do this before you decide that none of them are real?"

Jenny had already been frustrated by the inability to find someone genuine; Greg's pessimism was not helping her mood. "I'll do this as many times as Elanor wants me to." She turned away from Greg and consulted the list that she and Elanor had created. The next name was Susan Leichart, and her phone number was written down next to her name. As Jenny dialed the phone, she did hope for the best, although even she had to admit she wasn't very optimistic.

The following day while Greg was out running errands, Susan Leichart rang the doorbell right on time. Jenny was surprised to find that she looked more like a soccer mom than a stereotypical psychic. She was in her forties, had short brown hair, and was dressed in a basic shirt and khaki shorts. "Hi, I'm Susan Leichart," she said when Jenny opened the door.

"Jenny Watkins." The women shook hands, and much to Jenny's surprise, she got the distinct impression that Susan was for real. Jenny stood awestruck for a moment, leaving Susan hanging on the doorstep. Realizing she was being rude, Jenny shook her head rapidly, "Oh, I'm sorry. Please, come in."

"Thank you," Susan said, eyeballing Jenny suspiciously.

Feeling the need to explain, Jenny said, "You'll have to forgive me. I've had a lot of whack jobs over to the house lately, claiming to be psychic. Somehow I get the feeling you're actually legitimate."

Susan smiled knowingly. "Yes, I'm legitimate." She cocked her head to the side. "Tell me...why, exactly, did you call me?"

Jenny sighed, feeling an inexplicable need to be honest. "There have been some strange occurrences around here. I think someone might be trying to send a message, and I'm hoping you'll be able to tell me what that message is."

"What type of occurrences?"

Jenny hung her head. "Voices. I've been hearing voices."

"I see," Susan said in a strange tone. "So...what exactly do you think I'll be able to hear that you haven't been?"

Jenny wasn't sure what Susan was getting at. "I don't know. I was hoping you'd be able to tell me who is communicating with me. And why."

Susan had a maternal smile on her face, looking at Jenny as if she was a child who had just done something cute. "Tell me this, Jenny...how do you know I'm for real?"

Jenny shook her head. "I-I-I don't know." She shrugged her shoulders. "Intuition?"

"Well," Susan said, leaning forward and speaking in a whisper, "It takes a psychic to know a psychic."

It took a moment for Susan's message to sink in. Jenny's eyes widened and she took a step backward. "You're telling me I'm psychic?"

Susan smiled. "I could tell the moment we shook hands."

Jenny stood silently, paralyzed with shock. Thoughts swirled around her mind so rapidly she could focus on none of them. Susan broke the silence. "I take it this is your first time…"

Jenny only nodded.

Susan reached her hand out to Jenny's shoulder. "Come on," she said, "let's go inside, sit down, and we'll have a nice chat." She rubbed Jenny's back. "I'll tell you what," she joked, "I won't even charge you for my time."

Chapter 7

Jenny and Susan sat at the kitchen table, each with a glass of iced tea. "So," Susan said, grabbing the helm, "Why don't you tell me a little bit about these voices you've been hearing?"

"Actually," Jenny began, "It's only one voice. I hear it at night, right as I'm about to fall asleep."

"That makes sense," Susan observed.

"It does? Is that..." Jenny searched for the correct word. "*normal?*" As if any of this was normal.

Susan laughed knowingly. "Well, at night your mind is at rest, which enables the spirits the opportunity to take over." Susan shook her head and waved her hand as if to wipe the conversation clean. "This is how I've explained it to people in the past. The psychic mind is just a vehicle...like a car. You don't drive; someone else drives you. During the day, your mind is racing at a million miles an hour. It's as if your car is going really fast in circles. The spirits don't have the ability to get behind the wheel of a car that's constantly in motion...But...when you lie down to sleep at night, your mind slows down and eventually stops. Then the spirits are able to get behind the wheel and take you where they want to go.

"Now," Susan continued, "what happens when you hear the voice?"

"Well," Jenny recounted slowly, "it wakes me up. It scares me."

"That's understandable." Susan folded her hands on the table. "How much do you hear before you wake up?"

"Not a lot," Jenny confessed. "So far I've heard the name Steve O'dell twice, the name Elanor Whitby once, and the phrase *good day ma'am.*"

"Do those things mean anything?"

"Come to find out they do." Jenny recounted the history of the house, how she found Elanor, and the story of Elanor's relationship with Steve. "So what do you think it all means?"

Susan shrugged. "It's hard to tell. You'll need to allow the spirits a little more time to communicate before your mind starts racing again. It seems all they get to say is a word or two and you boot them out of the driver's seat."

"I guess I boot them out when I wake up?"

"Exactly. What you need to do—and it isn't easy—is learn to stay in that relaxed state, even after you've been contacted. I know hearing the voice is startling, but you need to resist the urge to jump into wakefulness."

"How do I do that?"

"Practice." Susan smiled. "It's easy for me now. At first, though, it was tough to do."

"When did you first discover you were a psychic?" Jenny asked.

"Back when I was a teenager. I kept having this recurring dream that I was a confederate soldier in the civil war. At first I thought it was too much homework getting to me, but the dreams seemed so *real.* And the same characters kept appearing in my dreams, over and over. I felt like I knew them. It's like the guys in my dream were my friends." Susan shook her head. "After a few months of that same recurring dream, I knew something was going on...something huge and amazing and scary. I knew these dreams were more than just dreams, but it took me a long time to confide that in anybody. I was afraid people would think I was losing it."

"Who did you tell?"

"A friend, of course. I was fifteen. I would always tell things to my friends first at that age. The funny thing is I didn't tell any of my best friends; I didn't think visions of confederate soldiers would fit very nicely into their lives, which centered mostly around boys and clothes at the time. Instead I told one of my lesser friends who I figured would be the most likely to take me seriously, and fortunately for me, she did. In fact, I only told her about the dreams. She's the one who suggested I might actually be a psychic receiving contact from one of those guys.

"She advised me to try to get the names of the soldiers in my dream, and I was able make a note of who they all were. I even found out the name of who I was. I'll never forget it. I was private first class Alexander Burkett. We did a little research, and we found out those people really existed. It took a lot of research, actually…there was no internet back then, keep in mind. But we were able to eventually find out that Alexander Burkett was killed in the battle of Antietam and was buried where he lay. A lot of those boys were." She lowered her eyes in sadness. "There were so many dead that they just buried some of them in trenches, all together. That's unimaginable to me. Those were people's *sons*." The look in Susan's eye led Jenny to believe she must have had a son of her own.

"Anyway," Susan continued, "there were efforts after the war to go back and identify all the soldiers and give them proper burials. Obviously, that would have been a daunting task, and some of those boys would inevitably be missed. It appears Alexander Burkett was one of the soldiers who got overlooked. His remains are still right there in the cornfield."

Jenny was mesmerized by her story. "So did you ever figure out why he contacted you?"

Susan sighed. "Well, he was never overt about it, but I figured he was suffering from unrest of some kind. Maybe he didn't know he was dead? Maybe he wanted to see his family again? Or maybe his girlfriend? I didn't know for sure. I just knew that anyone he might be looking for would be long dead by then, so if he wanted to find them, he'd need to cross over."

"Wow." Jenny said, "That's pretty intuitive for a fifteen year old."

"Well, I put a lot of thought into it. Those dreams were taking over my life. God, some of the things I saw in those dreams…" Susan shuddered. "I wouldn't wish that on anybody.

"Anyway, I eventually trained myself to have some control in my dreams. I knew I needed to get the message to Alexander that it would be okay to cross over. It took a lot of tries, but eventually it worked, and he did cross. And can I just tell you how amazing that was? When he reunited with his loved ones, it was one of the most unforgettable feelings I've ever experienced."

"I'll bet," Jenny replied, captivated.

"You know, I have found that reunion is one of the most powerful feelings you can experience. Even in this life, it's so emotional. Did you ever notice how much people love airports or watching footage of soldiers returning from deployment? That stuff can make you cry. You don't even have to know the people involved; you can still feel the power of their reunion.

"Well, the reunion phase is the best part of my job. On the cases where I guide someone to cross, I get to experience the joy they feel when they meet up with their loved ones again. And let me tell you, I sure felt *that* reunion." Susan locked eyes with Jenny, "I mean, imagine…Imagine how it felt to be Alexander, being separated from everyone he loved for over a hundred years. Imagine wandering around aimlessly like that—in limbo—not quite living, but not quite dead. He clearly wanted to see his loved ones, but he didn't know where to go to find them." Susan shook her head, as if she couldn't quite wrap her head around the thought of being that lost for that long.

"But then…" Susan's expression immediately changed, "Imagine the moment when you find everyone again. After all that time, you *finally* find your way home." She sat back in her chair, beaming. "Well, I felt that. I got to experience that joy with him." She let out a little laugh. "It made up for all of the horrors I had to witness, and all of the chaos his presence created in my life."

Jenny's blood ran cold at Susan's last statement. "What kind of chaos did he create?"

"Oh, God." Susan said. "It would be easier to list the aspects of my life that *didn't* get affected by Alexander." She sighed. "Well, first of all, I became reluctant to sleep. My dreams were so often about war, I reached the point where I didn't want to sleep at all anymore. I'd try to stay awake all night sometimes, which obviously had a profound effect on me. I lost a ton of weight. My grades went down dramatically—and suddenly—to the point where my parents accused me of doing drugs. In hindsight I wish I had just told them the truth, but the teenage brain is a strange creature indeed. I preferred my parents thinking I was a druggie to telling them I was having visions.

"But my circle of friends also changed. I started spending more and more time with Kelly—the girl I had confided in—and less time with the girls who had previously been my best friends. I spent my Friday and Saturday nights in the library with Kelly instead of at the mall with my old friends, who eventually wrote me off as being weird and started to want very little to do with me. It was okay with me, though, because at that point my focus had changed.

"The more I realized that my visions were true, the more I realized that I was not destined for a traditional life. Grades meant less to me because I figured I wouldn't be going to college anyway. If I truly had this gift, I wouldn't need college. The mall and boys and clothes and all of those other teenybopper obsessions seemed trivial compared to what I was dealing with." Susan let out another sigh. "That episode changed my whole perspective about life. Nothing was the same after Alexander."

For a brief moment, Jenny acknowledged to herself that nothing was going to be the same for her, either. Horrified at the prospect, she felt the need to change the subject in her own head. "So should I be trying to tell this…spirit…to cross over?"

"Not necessarily," Susan said. "Sometimes people contact you because they are trying to send a message. They're not lost—they know they're supposed to cross, but they don't want to until an issue gets resolved."

Jenny made a face and contemplated that last statement. "That would make sense here," she thought out loud. "Steve and Elanor's relationship was unresolved…"

Susan nodded. "Now this is by no means fact, since none of this is an exact science, but based on my own experiences—and the fact that Elanor said no one else could possibly know about the code-- I would surmise that the person contacting you is Steve, and he's trying to explain to Elanor what happened all those years ago. Since Elanor doesn't have the gift, he needs to use you as a go-between."

Jenny nodded slowly, deep in thought. She would love to be able to tell Elanor what happened and give her some peace in her final days. In order to do this, however, she would need to quickly master the art of receiving messages. She wasn't sure just how much time Elanor had left.

"So…what exactly do I need to do in order to allow the spirits to communicate with me?"

"Well, first you need to *expect* periodic contact," Susan said. "That should be easier now that you know you have the gift. Correct me if I'm wrong, but until now you've been surprised by the voice every time you've heard it."

"That's an understatement."

Susan laughed. "Well, now you are aware that it can happen, so hopefully you won't be quite as shocked by it. And now that you know that the spirits are most likely to make contact when your mind is at rest, you can get a feel for *when* to expect it. You can even facilitate it, or at least try to, by achieving that state of relaxation during the day. There's no guarantee that if you meditate you'll get contacted, but you can pretty much guarantee that you *won't* get contacted if your mind is buzzing a mile a minute.

"And," Susan continued, "you also need to understand that the spirits can't hurt you. Now, don't get me wrong, you are going to be exposed to some disturbing visions. You may hear messages that are a lot less pleasant than the ones you've been hearing. You may feel pain—excruciating physical pain—but be aware that it only lasts the duration of the vision. It isn't your pain that you're feeling—you are feeling vicarious pain to give you a better understanding of what the spirit has endured."

Seeing that Jenny looked rather uncomfortable, Susan continued. "Now I told you before that you're not in charge of the visions, but I don't mean to imply that you have no control. While you can't control when you get a vision or how long your vision lasts, you can control how *short* it is. In fact, you've been doing that already." Susan reached out her hand and held Jenny's. "If ever a vision gets to be too much, you have the ability to snap yourself out of it. After you become seasoned you'll probably find that you don't ever want to snap yourself out of a vision, no matter how awful, simply because the most awful visions are usually the most telling. But until you get a handle on this gift, only do what you're comfortable with. It *is* a gift, but if not handled properly, it can feel like a curse."

Jenny rubbed her eyes with her free hand. "I'm so glad you are here telling me all of this."

Susan smiled. "I'm actually very happy to do it. I am still friends with Kelly, the girl who first helped me with my gift, and I am glad to be able to finally pay it forward." She let go of Jenny's hand.

"*I'm a psychic,*" Jenny stated with disbelief. "You'll have to forgive me, but this is an awful lot to swallow. This conversation has just turned my entire life upside down."

"I know," Susan said, "which is why I want you to program my phone number into your phone. Please, please, please feel free to call me any time, day or night, if you need anything at all. I know some of the things you can experience are disturbing or downright scary, so if you need some help sorting it out, or even just to vent, please call."

"I don't want to call you in the middle of the night," Jenny said.

"Oh, don't worry about that. Half my visions come to me in the form of dreams, so I often get out of bed at 3 a.m. to write down everything I experienced. My husband is used to it by now. He says it's like being married to an OBGYN who's constantly on call."

"So your husband is on board with the idea of you being psychic?"

"Oh, sure," Susan said. "But I already knew I was psychic when I met him. He actually found it fascinating. I think it was part of the attraction."

"But what about other people?" Jenny was dancing around what she really wanted to say, which was *my husband thinks I'm crazy.* "When you tell people you are a psychic, do most of them believe you?"

"Some do, some don't. I actually don't care if people believe me. My clients believe me, which is the important thing. My gift has been able to provide a lot of people with answers, and that's been very rewarding. If other people don't believe me, that's their problem."

Jenny let out a little laugh, jealous of both Susan's and Elanor's ability to not care. Perhaps that did come with age…

"So what you should do is give yourself time to relax," Susan concluded as she stood up. "Quiet your mind. Expect some sort of contact, and stay relaxed when you hear it. Allow the spirit to say more than just a few words, and hopefully you'll get some answers."

"Thank you," Jenny replied, also standing. "I'll definitely try that."

The women walked to the front door and exchanged phone numbers. Jenny thanked Susan for all of her help and waited on the front step until Susan drove away. Awestruck, Jenny resumed her place back at the kitchen table, sipped some more tea, and tried to contemplate everything she had just learned. She was *psychic.* She had always regarded herself as ordinary in every sense of the word, but now she was aware of this rare and valuable gift that would allow her to help people in unimaginable ways. She knew she would eventually be proud of this development, but for now she was just shocked by it.

Greg came home from his errands to find Jenny sitting somewhat statuesque at the table, clearly unnerved. "Is something wrong?" he immediately asked.

Jenny was reluctant to tell this news to the man who had been only minimally supportive. She braced herself for ridicule and proceeded. "I do believe the psychic I met with today was real."

"Oh yeah?" Greg asked. "How can you tell?"

"That's the thing...I just kind of knew." She looked up at Greg to gauge his reaction. "It appears psychics can recognize other psychics."

After a moment of consideration, he replied, "So you're saying you're psychic? Is that what this woman told you?" Based on Greg's neutral tone, Jenny was unable to assess what he was thinking.

"Yes, and it does make sense, if you think about it. I have been hearing voices...voices that, apparently, no one else can hear. And I didn't tell you before, because I was afraid you would think I was completely crazy, but the voice told me the phrase *good day ma'am.* That was Elanor and Steve's code for *I love you.* When I visited with Elanor, she told me that nobody could have possibly known that." Jenny swallowed hard, hoping Greg would believe her. "Susan—the psychic—seems to believe Steve is contacting me, trying to deliver a message to Elanor before she dies."

Greg remained expressionless. "Well, what do you know?"

Jenny waited for elaboration that didn't come. Was that it? Was that all the reaction she was going to get from Greg? After a bombshell like the one she just dropped, she expected *some* kind of response. After several moments of awkward silence, Jenny said, "Well, I think I'm going to go upstairs and take a bath."

"Take a bath?" Greg asked, looking at the clock. "It's kind of a weird time for a bath, isn't it? The middle of the afternoon? I was actually hoping we could get a little more work done around here. It doesn't seem like you accomplished much while I was gone."

And there it was, Jenny thought. She discovered she had a life-altering gift, yet because she hadn't pried up any floorboards while he was out, she *hadn't accomplished much.* Anger once again began to simmer within her, but she made the concerted effort to dismiss it, knowing the impact it would have on her ability to fully relax.

"I know it's weird, but I'm a little spooked by what Susan had to say. I just need a little time to regroup, and then I'll be able to help out with the house."

"Well, I'll be down here working," Greg commented. "Come join me when you're done."

Aware of the dig that had just been made but choosing to ignore it, Jenny headed eagerly up to the bathroom. She had bigger things to worry about than whether or not Greg approved of her afternoon bath. She needed to quiet her mind, so she tried to think of all of the things that would facilitate relaxation. She put some soft music on the radio, turned off the lights, lit some scented candles, and added bubbles to her bath. She undressed and climbed into the tub, feeling the warmth envelop her. She laid her head back against the tub, breathing deeply, clearing the thoughts from her head. She closed her eyes, trying to live entirely in the moment. The sounds of the bubbles popping around her and her rhythmic breath were nearly hypnotic; however, despite her best efforts, she failed to hear any voices. Eventually the water around her became cold, and she decided it was time to get out of the tub.

A little disappointed but undeterred, she hoped the evening would bring about a different story. In the meantime she dressed and threw herself mercilessly into the renovation project. Her goal was to make herself good and tired, figuring this would enable her to fully relax at bed time. Her plan worked; by nightfall, she was completely exhausted and looking quite forward to climbing into bed.

Her muscles ached as she slid between the sheets. She thoroughly enjoyed the feeling of resting her head on the pillow. As waves of relaxation came over her, she once again heard the voice.

"Lake Wimsat."

Her eyes popped open. "Dammit!" she whispered out loud. She had woken up too soon, but she was excited to hear a different message. She decided at that moment that she would pay a visit to

Elanor in the morning to see the significance of Lake Wimsat. While she knew a phone call would have sufficed, she wanted to get out of the house. She also knew that Greg may not have been too excited about her plan, but she didn't care.

Perhaps she was going to reach the mindset of a forty year old a little ahead of schedule.

Chapter 8

Jenny knocked quietly on Elanor's door; once again, Elanor looked delighted to see her. "Oh, hello, dear! Please, come in! Do you have any exciting news to tell me?" She looked like a kid at Christmas.

Jenny walked over to Elanor's bed proudly. "Yes, in fact, this time I do."

"Well let's hear it!" Elanor said.

Jenny laughed. "Okay, here goes. I met with a few psychics, but they were frauds."

"Bastards."

"But then I met with Susan Leichart, and she was real." Jenny recounted the conversation between her and Susan, with Elanor hanging on every word. "Susan seems to think the person communicating with me is Steve, and he wants to get a message to you." Jenny left off the part about having limited time to do so.

"I wonder what that message is!" Elanor declared enthusiastically; this was clearly the first exciting thing to happen to her in a long time.

"Well," Jenny began, "I heard another message last night, but unfortunately I wasn't able to stay relaxed enough to hear very much. All I heard was *Lake Wimsat.*"

Elanor clapped her hands together. "Oh, Lake Wimsat. Steve and I spent so much time there." Her face looked elated. "It was a safe place for us to go. We had found this little out-of-the-way spot where no one ever went." She laughed. "We had to climb through some pretty thick brush to get there, but it was worth it. There was a big, flat rock that looked out over the lake, and because it was so far off the beaten path nobody ever bothered us. We had no chance of being caught when we were there, so we were able to act like a couple." Elanor gave Jenny an exaggerated wink. "But it wasn't all about sex. We spent a lot of time there just cuddling. In fact, that rock is where we came up with our plans to change the world." Elanor looked distant again. "Oh, yes…Lake Wimsat."

"Can you think of any reason why I would hear that?"

Elanor made an intent face as she thought about it. "No, not anything in particular. Not off the top of my head, anyway. But Lake Wimsat played a bigger role in my life than just that. Once I made enough money from the magazine, I had a house built on the lake. It wasn't near where Steve and I used to hang out, but on the other side. They weren't developing on that side of the lake with it being part of a state park and all." Realizing she was beginning a tangent, she switched gears and said, "I spent almost forty years in that house. Who's to say what event we're supposed to be focusing on? "

Jenny was upset with herself for waking too soon. Perhaps if she could have stayed relaxed, the message would have been much clearer. "Well, I'll try to see if I can come up with anything more specific. Unfortunately I don't have much control over when I receive messages."

"That's okay, dear. I don't expect you to have all the answers. I'll try to think if anything remarkable happened at the lake. It'll give me something to do until you come back."

"Well, hopefully I'll be back soon." Jenny put her purse strap over her shoulder.

With a heartbreaking look of disappointment, Elanor said, "You know, you don't have to leave right away."

Jenny thought about Greg working on the house by himself. With the forty minute drive to Lumberton, she had already been gone over an hour. It would be close to two hours by the time she got back if she left right away. However, she didn't feel the need to go rushing home. Every part of her wanted to stay and talk to Elanor, so Jenny set her purse down on the floor and said, "What would you like to chat about?"

A contented smile splayed across Elanor's face. "I want to talk about you a little bit. I feel like you know a lot more about me than I do about you."

"Okay," Jenny said with an apprehensive smile.

"So, for starters…how long have you lived in that house?"

"Not long. Only a couple of weeks."

"Where did you move from?"

"Kentucky."

"Wow. That's quite a long move." Elanor made a face. "I'm sure there were a few houses in Kentucky that needed some repair. What made you choose *that* house?"

"Well," Jenny began, "My husband Greg has always had this dream of fixing up a luxury home. His father used to do that when Greg was a teenager, and he always helped his father out. He learned a lot about fixing up houses that way, so even though he's a teacher by trade, he still knows a thing or two about renovation.

"We looked for some nice houses to fix up in Kentucky, but there were no houses with as much potential as your old house. Not within our price range, anyway. Your house was by far the most house we could get for our money, probably because it's not in an affluent neighborhood. Most luxury homes, no matter how run-down, were out of our price range simply because of the neighborhood they were in."

"Did *you* have dreams of fixing up a house?"

"Honestly?" Jenny replied. "Not really. That was always my husband's dream; I just wanted to see it come true for him."

"So you moved all the way from Kentucky to fulfill your husband's dream? That's pretty big of you."

Jenny smiled, glad somebody recognized that.

"So what's *your* dream, dear?" Elanor asked.

"My dream?" Jenny sat back in her chair. "My dream…" She racked her brain, but she really couldn't come up with anything. "I guess I don't have one."

"Everybody has a dream," Elanor said sweetly. "You just haven't thought about it enough yet. Perhaps you haven't given yourself permission to. I think a person's dreams say a lot about them. When I meet someone new I often like to ask them this question, simply because I think the answer is very telling. You ready?"

"Shoot."

"If money was no object, and people couldn't tell you no, what would you be doing with your life?"

A thought which was too embarrassing to reveal popped into Jenny's head immediately. Elanor, able to read Jenny's face, continued. "Come on, say it. Don't be shy. What, do you think I'm going to laugh at you or something? If that's the case, then I know for sure you've never read my magazine."

Jenny felt her face flush; she had indeed never read an issue of *Choices*, and she was horribly ashamed to admit it.

"I'll forgive you for not reading my magazine if you tell me what your dream is."

Jenny giggled and sighed with defeat. "Well, this past week my dream has been to pursue this voice I've been hearing." She looked at her lap. "Now that I know I have some kind of psychic ability, I'd love to delve into that."

"Well that seems simple enough."

"Not really," Jenny admitted. "My husband hasn't exactly been as supportive as I'd like."

"Oh? How so?"

"Well, he kind of gives me a hard time about it. He thinks I should be focusing on the renovation, and whenever I take a break from that to investigate the voice, he feels like I'm not meeting my responsibilities."

Elanor lowered her eyebrows. "Well, that's a little bit shitty, don't you think?"

Jenny didn't react outwardly, but inside her spirit soared. "What do you mean?" she asked, desperate to hear someone else say what she was ashamed to be feeling.

"You moved all the way to Kentucky to pursue his dream, and then he's giving you a hard time about pursuing yours? That doesn't seem right. Besides, his dream is just to make a house look pretty. Anybody can do that. I don't know anyone who can do what you do."

Jenny nodded slightly, feeling both validated and ashamed at the same time. Her dream was just as important as Greg's...if not more so...but she was quite sure that equality would never be recognized. In her marriage Greg clearly called the shots, a notion which was suddenly disgraceful in Jenny's mind.

"Pick up an issue of *Choices*," Elanor continued. "You'll change your tune. It'll give you the kick in the pants you need to stand up for yourself." Elanor patted Jenny's hand.

Eager to change the subject, Jenny asked, "Miss Elanor, do you mind if I ask you a question?"

"Of course not. Fire away."

"How did the house come to be in such a state of disrepair?"

Elanor chuckled guiltily. "Well, my parents lived there their whole lives. My father passed away first, and then my mother a few years later. When my mother died, she left everything to me, but by that time I'd made a bunch of money for myself, and I was already living on Lake Wimsat. I didn't need that house. I didn't want that house. I didn't want any of my father's money, even though I got it all." She got a diabolical grin on her face. "Do you know what I did with the house and all that money?"

Jenny just knew this was going to be good. "What did you do?"

"The first thing I did was give the house away. I just signed it over, furniture and all, to a low income family. I wanted to give a family an opportunity at privilege that they would never have had otherwise. I didn't take into account that a low income family wouldn't have the means to maintain such an expensive home. I guess it didn't really turn out to be much of a gift." Elanor laughed. "Here, low income family, here's a house with inordinately high heating and cooling bills and super-expensive custom everything that will cost a fortune to replace. Enjoy."

"It was a nice idea."

"Hey, I tried. What can I say?" Elanor continued. "Now as far as all that money goes, I got to thinking about a stupid monologue my father threw at me every chance he got. I swear I heard it at least once a week." Elanor tucked her chin into her chest, lowered her eyebrows, and deepened her voice. *"Whitby money has been in our family for generations. Samuel Whitby was the first Whitby on American soil, and he made a fortune in tobacco, blah blah blah."* Elanor resumed her natural voice. "Well, it doesn't take a genius to figure out that somebody who made a fortune growing tobacco in the south in the 1700s did so through the use of slaves. He got rich on hard work, alright, but not his own. The way I saw it, the descendants of his slaves deserved the money, not me. I tried to track down who his slaves had been so I could follow their lineage, but I had no luck. So instead I took that money—every damn bit of it—and donated it to the United Negro College Fund. I figured it was a good-enough second-best." Elanor began to giggle. "Can you imagine what my father's reaction would have been to know that all that Whitby money was given away...as a *handout*...to *black people*? He'd have shit his pants if he knew. In fact, I bet he's rolling over in his grave right now just because I'm talking about it.

"Oh, look at me, talking about myself again. I want to learn a little something about you."

"I'm not as interesting as you are," Jenny admitted.

"Are you kidding? You're a psychic. I just wrote shit in a magazine."

"I've only been a psychic for, like, four days."

"But you were interesting before that. Everybody's interesting if you ask them the right questions." Elanor eyed Jenny up and down. "Let me see...are you a traveler? Been anywhere exciting?"

Jenny giggled. "Does Detroit count?"

"No. Detroit most definitely does not count. Not unless you were a pole dancer or a CIA agent while you were there."

"I was visiting my grandmother."

"Was your grandmother a CIA agent?"

"No. But she did like to make quilts."

"Okay, we're not getting anywhere with this." Elanor managed to keep her tone serious, but Jenny couldn't keep the laughter in. "Talent," Elanor continued. "Do you have some kind of hidden talent?"

Jenny felt her face redden as she lowered her eyes and shrugged her shoulders.

"Aha!" Elanor proclaimed victoriously. "I got it, didn't I? So what's this hidden talent you have? Are you a singer?"

Jenny shook her head. "No, I can't carry a tune in a bucket, but I have been known to paint. I'm not sure how good I am, though..."

"Good is in the eye of the beholder," Elanor stated. "I'll tell you what...I've been to some museums that have housed million dollar paintings, and all I see is crap. It looks to me like somebody spilled some paint on a canvas and forgot to clean it up. But, clearly, to some people those paintings are exquisite." She shrugged her shoulders. "So what do you paint?"

"Landscapes, mostly."

"Landscapes. Now, that I can get into. Do your trees look like trees, or are they purple and upside down?"

"I do my best to make my pictures lifelike."

"Then I'm sure I would like your paintings. And I'm sure you are much more talented than I am in that regard. I can't even draw a stick figure with legs the same length. Do you have your paintings hanging around your house?"

"No," Jenny confessed. "When Greg and I moved in together, we used his furniture since it was better. The pictures clashed with his furniture, so we didn't hang them."

"It sounds to me like you need new furniture."

"I think making new paintings would be more affordable."

"Well then get to it."

Jenny smiled, realizing at that moment how much she did miss painting. She hadn't put a brush to canvas in ages, and a pang of longing grew inside her. Although, with the renovation in full swing, she knew her painting supplies would have to be packed up a while longer.

Elanor and Jenny continued to talk for another hour, laughing and carrying on as if they'd known each other for ages. Eventually, Elanor started to look tired, so Jenny said goodbye and headed out to her car. As soon as she closed the car door behind her and was officially alone, an unanticipated wave of emotion swept over her. Tears welled up in her eyes as she turned the key and backed out of her parking spot.

Elanor had struck a copious amount of nerves during that conversation. The feelings Jenny had tried to keep buried down inside were now exposed and raw. She had lost herself, and now she'd been called on it. Somewhere along the line she stopped being Jenny and started being Greg's wife. Greg's wife didn't paint. Greg's wife didn't hang her paintings if they clashed with his furniture. Greg's wife moved to Georgia so he could renovate a house.

Greg's wife wasn't a psychic.

Tears drenched Jenny's cheeks as she drove, trying to figure out when, exactly, she stopped existing. If she had to pinpoint a moment, it would have been when the star running back of the college football team turned to her and said hello in World History class. She remembered the exhilaration of being noticed by such an attractive, popular and athletic guy. She had always been so nondescript in her own mind; she couldn't imagine what prompted him to talk to her. Realizing she'd have very few qualities that would have actually impressed him, she made sure that conversation—and every conversation thereafter—focused on him.

"That was it," Jenny said out loud to no one. "That was why he liked me." Greg didn't like her because of her intelligence, sense of humor, or her artistic ability, she mused. He liked her because, with her, he always got to talk about his favorite topic of conversation— himself. As their relationship progressed, she always agreed to go where he wanted to go. She always agreed to do what he wanted to do. She always marveled about how wonderful he was, spending very little time talking about herself. "He doesn't love me," Jenny said through sobs. "He loves the fact that I worship him."

Realizing her ability to drive had been greatly impaired by her flood of emotion, Jenny pulled over into a bank parking lot and stopped her car. She sobbed freely into her hands, leaning her forehead onto the steering wheel. "I could have been anybody," she cried. "He picked me because I didn't matter."

Her crying maintained its intensity for several minutes until slowly she began to regain control. She breathed deeply and eventually the tears stopped falling. She leaned her head back against the seat of her car feeling exhausted and drained, but markedly better since the release of all of that bottled up emotion. She reached for a tissue she kept in her purse and cleaned herself off, although her eyes remained red and puffy. With one last deep breath, she put her car into reverse and continued her drive home.

She didn't allow herself to think anymore as she traveled. She felt a peace within her, realizing she had a lot more thinking to do, but resolving to save it for another time. As she approached Evansdale, her driving was little more than automatic; then she caught herself taking a right when she should have taken a left.

She knew what was happening. She was being taken somewhere, and she knew she needed to maintain her trance-like state in order to reach her unknown destination. She did not allow the excitement of the experience to distract her; her emotional emptiness was hugely helpful in that regard. She simply didn't have the energy to become elevated.

The car took what seemed to be automatic lefts and rights until Jenny ended up on a country road she had never seen been before. She drove down to the end of a cul-de-sac where a lone house stood a good distance off the road; she knew this was her destination.

She turned the car off and climbed out, walking somewhat zombie-like into the expansive front yard. She closed her eyes, and she was able to see this house as just a frame. The grass didn't exist and the mature trees were gone, replaced instead by freshly-churned dirt and rocks. She opened her eyes and the house fell into place like an overlay against the vision of its frame, with the grass and trees back in place. She closed her eyes once again saw a gray haired man walking across the barren soil toward her.

"Hey, thanks for coming out so early on a Saturday morning," the gray-haired man said.

"No problem." A deep voice resonated through Jenny; she knew her character—presumably Steve--was speaking. "I've got nothing else going on. So what's the story?"

"I came out last night because I'd forgotten to pack up one of my tools, and I noticed one of the structural beams is rotted and cracked. I wanted you to take a look at it before we did anything else. I'd do it myself, but this damn hip of mine won't let me get up on that ladder. You seem to know your shit better than anyone else on the crew, so I want you to climb up there and tell me how bad it is. I think we need to replace the Goddamn thing, but that's going to mean a lot of extra work. It was one of the first boards we put up."

"Okay," the deep voice replied, "I'll take a look at that for you."

The gray-haired man gestured with his hand, inviting Jenny to approach the house first. As the view changed behind Jenny's closed eyes, shifting focus from the man to the house, the deafening bang of a gunshot rang out, followed by an intense, searing pain in the back of Jenny's head.

She instantly placed her hands on her head, expecting to feel a large, gaping wound and oozing blood. There was no wound, no blood, and no more pain. She opened her eyes to find the grass had returned, and the house once again had walls, shutters, and plants in hanging baskets. Jenny's heart raced and her hands shook as she stood alone in a seemingly innocuous suburban yard. However, she knew this wasn't just an idyllic yard; this had been a crime scene. Elanor's father hadn't blackmailed Steve into leaving town; Steve had been murdered, right there at the construction site by a gray-haired man he'd regarded as a friend.

Chapter 9

Jenny made a note of the house number and climbed back into her car. She allowed the air conditioning to hit her face for a moment before driving, providing her with much-needed clarity and sobriety. As she drove back out the way she came, she searched for a street sign to indicate where she was. Eventually an intersection informed her that she was on Meadowbrook Road, which she jotted down on the back of a receipt from her purse.

Unaware of where she was with respect to her own house, she typed in her address and allowed her GPS to guide her home. She knew Greg was going to be less than thrilled with her when she arrived, but she didn't have enough energy to care.

As she walked through the door of her house, Greg was patching holes in the drywall where phone jacks had once been. "Let me guess," he said without looking at her, "you were visiting Elanor."

"Yup," Jenny remarked casually. She walked into the kitchen, dropped her purse on the counter, and then headed upstairs to the laptop.

She could hear the heavy sighs of Greg's disapproval, but they had no impact on her. She was still emotionally void, and she actually enjoyed the numbness. She knew she would ordinarily be feeling insubordinate at that moment, and the inability to feel anything was a welcome replacement.

She opened her laptop and pulled the receipt out of her pocket. Using the county's website, she typed in the address on Meadowbrook Road to see when the house had been constructed. The house was completed in 1954 by Larrabee and Sons Custom Home Builders and purchased by the original owners shortly after.

Unable to remember exactly when Elanor had been born, Jenny searched for her name, eliciting the same results she had found last time. She clicked on the helpful website from before, confirming Elanor had been born in 1934. That would have put her at twenty while this house was being constructed, which was the age she claimed to be when Steve disappeared.

Part of her wanted to get back into her car and drive immediately to Maple Estates, but she had left because Elanor was becoming tired. She, too, was exhausted, so she decided to make the drive the next morning. Knowing full well that Greg wanted Jenny to come back downstairs and help him, she instead climbed into bed, let out a big sigh, and drifted quickly off to sleep.

Elanor's face had turned a pale shade of green, worrying Jenny tremendously. "But I could be wrong," Jenny added quickly. "It was just a vision. I may have made the whole thing up."

"No. No you didn't," Elanor said weakly. "I remember the house on Meadowbrook Road. That was where Steve was working last. I went there that Monday morning looking for answers." Elanor covered her heart with her hands. "I feel like I'm going to be sick."

"I'm so sorry, Elanor. I didn't mean to upset you. Maybe I shouldn't have told you."

"No, I'm glad you did. I wanted answers, and now I have them." She appeared dazed as she spoke. "I just never would have imagined that would be the answer I'd get."

Jenny looked sympathetically at Elanor, knowing all too well how it felt to have her foundation rocked to the core; Susan's pronouncement had the same effect on Jenny a few days earlier. She wished she could take Elanor's pain away, but she knew nothing she could say would provide any relief. Riddled with helplessness and guilt, Jenny felt almost as if she had killed Steve herself.

"And now I have a whole new set of questions," Elanor added.

"I know. I'm sure they're the same questions I've been asking myself. I was actually hoping you might have some of the answers."

Elanor shook her head slowly. "I don't know the gray-haired man's name, if that's what you're looking for."

"I don't suppose there's any way that man was your father and I just saw things wrong…"

"No," Elanor said, "My father went straight from brown to bald. There was never any gray. Besides, he wouldn't have had any reason to meet Steve at a construction site."

"I know," Jenny admitted. "I'm grasping at straws."

"I am still positive my father was behind it, though," Elanor declared. "I'm quite sure he paid off this gray-haired guy. Typical Luther Whitby…he didn't have the balls to do the dirty work himself. I just wonder who that guy was who actually did it."

"It appeared to be the foreman of the construction site."

Elanor looked angry. "The same piece of shit who told me that Steve left town…he did have gray hair, that asshole." With a furrowed brow, she added, "But why would he do it?"

"Isn't it obvious?"

Elanor chuckled. "Yeah, of course he got paid. But I'd like to think that most people wouldn't commit murder for money. What made this guy willing to kill someone for a couple of bucks?"

Jenny shook her head. "I don't know."

"I'd love to find out."

"Well, I'll see what I can do," Jenny said. "I'll do a little research for you and see what I can come up with."

Elanor smiled lovingly at Jenny. "You truly are a doll, you know that?"

"Thanks, Miss Elanor. You know, I was thinking…there is one…" Jenny made a face, unsure of the correct word, "*positive* thing to come out of this."

Wordlessly, Elanor lifted her eyes in Jenny's direction.

"Your whole life you wondered how Steve could have left you. But it turns out he didn't. He was taken from you."

A half-hearted smile graced Elanor's lips. "I guess he didn't leave me, did he?"

"No, ma'am. And I'm hoping you'll be able to take some solace in that."

The smile faded from Elanor's face, replaced with a look of deep reflection. "Over the years I have often wondered where he was—what he was doing. Even though I missed him, I always hoped he was happy. I took pleasure in believing he was out there changing some piece of the world in his own way. I never imagined his life

73

would have been cut so short. He was a good man. He didn't deserve that."

"No one deserves that," Jenny agreed softly.

Elanor let out a deep breath. "I guess I underestimated a lot of the people in my life. I should have known Steve wouldn't have betrayed me. I knew him better than that." Elanor smoothed her sheets as she looked down at her lap. "And I guess my father was an even bigger asshole than I thought."

Jenny felt positively horrible. Her abilities were supposed to be helping Elanor; instead she had just made things immeasurably worse. She stayed by Elanor's bedside for the remainder of the afternoon, consoling her until the conversation eventually turned lighter. By the time Jenny headed home, Elanor's spirits had elevated to the point where Jenny felt she could be left alone. It wasn't until Jenny was in her car that she allowed her own tears to flow. Had she made a terrible mistake by disclosing her vision? She knew only one person in the world could answer that for her.

Chapter 10

Jenny sat at Susan's kitchen table, the smell of bacon still lingering in the air. "I'm really not sure I did the right thing," Jenny concluded. She lowered her eyes to meet the stare of Buddy, Susan's overweight—and overzealous—beagle, whose eyes were bulging out of his head. Jenny wasn't entirely sure what spectacular trick Buddy was expecting her to do.

"You did," Susan replied confidently. "Steve wanted you to have the vision. It's a piece of information Elanor was supposed to have for some reason." Susan blew on her coffee and took a sip. "You're not the driver, remember? You don't get to choose what the messages are. It's your job just to deliver them. Maybe the purpose of the vision was to set the record straight about her father—get her to realize exactly what his true colors really were."

Jenny sighed. "But that only made her feel worse." Jenny reached down and scratched Buddy's ears. "I guess I envisioned myself telling Elanor things that would make her happy. I never imagined I'd be relaying such sad news."

"Oh, it's not always happy, that's for sure," Susan declared emphatically. "In fact, it usually isn't." With a sigh, she added, "I remember once I had to tell a grieving set of parents that their murdered teenage daughter had been exchanging sex for drugs." She shook her head in a near shudder. "I had teenagers myself at the time, and I almost couldn't bring myself to do it. It was like adding insult to injury in the worst possible way.

"But it was a message the daughter wanted them to have. Once the toxicology reports came back on her body, her parents would have been made aware of the high levels of heroin in her system anyway. She wanted her parents to know that she didn't blame them for her drug use. She regarded them as good parents. She only got into drugs because she was bored and had a little too much money for her own good. She never meant to hurt her parents, and she was sorry for the anguish she had caused them."

"I can't imagine having to tell her parents that."

"Like I said, I almost didn't. But it explained why she was murdered, so I had to tell them. It wasn't a random act of violence like everyone suspected. She had been promising sex to drug dealers and then not delivering. Her rape and strangulation was nothing more than an act of revenge on the part of the drug dealers."

"Dear Lord," Jenny replied. "I guess this girl didn't know what she was getting into."

"Not at all."

"How did her parents take it?"

"They told me to fuck off."

Jenny winced.

"But," Susan continued, "when the toxicology report did come back, I'm sure a small piece of them felt some understanding. That's what you have to realize. It's not your job to deliver happy endings to people; it's your job to make the unhappy endings make sense. I think people take comfort when they can piece things together, no matter how disturbing the puzzle. It's the missing pieces that cause people the most anguish."

"I feel like I handed Elanor some pieces but took away others. Now she wants to know who that gray-haired man was."

"Well, at least she has the correct pieces this time. The picture is becoming a little bit clearer."

"The picture is uglier than she ever imagined."

"It usually is."

"We need to talk about this." Greg stood with his arms folded as Jenny poured herself a glass of water. She headed for the medicine cabinet; her primary concern was to relieve the headache that had started at Susan's house.

76

Unlike every moment in the past when Greg spoke to her in a disapproving tone, Jenny felt remarkably unabashed. "Talk about what?"

"You know what I mean. You disappearing every chance you get to go play cops and robbers."

"Cops and robbers, huh?" Jenny was surprised by her own indifference. She swallowed two tablets with a long drink of water and added, "I suppose this is the point in the conversation where I'm supposed to apologize."

"What is with you?" Greg asked. "You have been dogging your responsibilities since we moved in here, and now you're getting a bitchy attitude with me."

"Correct me if I'm wrong, but you just called what I'm doing *cops and robbers.* That's not exactly amicable. But I guess it's okay for you to be condescending with me, just not the other way around."

Greg threw up his hands in disbelief. "I can't believe you're acting like this. It's like you've become a totally different person since we moved here."

"You know what? I have." Jenny made eye contact. "And I like it." She walked past him to the formal living room.

Greg followed her to the doorway. "What the hell are you doing?"

"Renovating." This time it was Jenny's turn to respond without looking. She picked up her putty knife and started to scrape at the wallpaper. "I figure since I have some free time, I'll help you."

"Unbelievable," Greg muttered as he walked away. Jenny looked at the open doorway where Greg had just been standing, her smile so broad it rivaled her happiest moment. She returned to her scraping, eager to busy her mind with trivial tasks. As selfish as it seemed, for the next few hours she needed to not be psychic. Ideally, she wouldn't even have had to be a wife.

She found herself looking very forward to Greg's bachelor party weekend back in Kentucky. Three days without Greg seemed like a vacation; a lifetime without him would have been even better.

Later that night, Jenny sat in a guest bedroom, surrounded by six of her favorite paintings. She admired each one, periodically reaching out to touch their surfaces. Her fingers traced along the path of a river in a painting she'd made after her freshman year of college.

With the weight of her final exams behind her, she'd relished heading off to the water's edge each day to work on that painting in solitude. With the sun on her back and the birds chirping in the background, she'd felt invincible when she made that scene.

A second painting featured an autumn landscape with a mountain in the background. Creating this piece had provided her with solace when one of her dearest friends had moved away near the end of high school. Jenny smiled as she touched the spot on the mountain that had actually been a mistake but turned out to look better than her original intent. She remembered thinking at the time that she needed to allow herself to venture from the plan more often, but that wasn't in her nature. Once she had an idea of how the painting should look, she only deviated by accident. Going forward, she decided in the guest bedroom, she would paint more freely; perhaps she could surprise herself with ability she didn't know she had.

She turned to a third painting of a meadow, noting the golden-honey color of the wheat in the foreground. She had made this painting simply because she felt like it, which invoked a smile in her. She didn't need a reason to paint. She enjoyed it, and that was reason enough.

After deliberating each of the remaining paintings, she delicately rewrapped five of them and put them back into storage. She left the sixth leaning against the guest bedroom wall, admiring it one last time before she walked away.

The following day Jenny's task was to remove the quarter round from all of the baseboards so the floor could eventually be replaced. While the task wasn't difficult, the constant crouching and gripping of the tool made her stiff and sore. By the time she had completed the upstairs and part of the downstairs, she was in desperate need of a break.

In the foyer she stopped to stand up and stretch for a moment. "You have three minutes to tell me why the fuck you're here, and then I'm calling the police."

The male voice was unfamiliar, so Jenny closed her eyes, trying to remain calm and still. A bald man in a sport coat materialized before her, looking very angry. The same voice from the construction site resonated through Jenny. "I'm here because I love your daughter. I want to iron out any differences you and I have because I'd like to propose to her, and I want to do it with your blessing."

The bald man let out a laugh. "You might as well just leave now, because you'll never get my blessing."

"Sir, I want you to know I wasn't taking advantage of Elanor. I truly love her, more than I've ever loved anybody else. I want to show you and the rest of the world that my intentions are honest. I want to be able to be with her freely instead of having to sneak around. I'm tired of sneaking around. I want to marry her, sir."

"Over my dead body."

Jenny felt frustration and disappointment building inside her. "Let me say this differently. I *am* going to propose to her, and I do believe she will say yes. I'd like to have you on board with the idea."

"There is no way in hell my daughter is going to marry you."

"She's twenty, sir. She can make her own decisions."

The bald man stuck his finger in Jenny's face. "Now you listen to me. My daughter is *not* going to marry you. Do you hear?"

"No sir."

The bald man lowered his finger and gritted his teeth. "You don't know who you're messing with." The psychotic look in his eye would have frightened most people, but Jenny didn't feel fear.

"I'm sorry this didn't go better, sir." Jenny felt herself growing distant, knowing this was the point the two men parted ways. She opened her eyes slowly, leery that she would still see the angry bald man in her foyer, but the entryway was empty. She ran her fingers through her hair and shivered, still spooked by the notion of what was happening to her.

A debate ensued in Jenny's head. She wanted to report her findings Elanor immediately, but she knew she had been pushing her luck at home. Although she was discovering how fundamentally lopsided her marriage was, she had agreed to be a partner in the renovation, and she had to admit she was being much less involved than she had promised. She decided to finish the quarter round removal before she headed to Maple Estates that evening. Still sore but newly motivated, she got back on her hands and knees and continued.

Chapter 11

Jenny walked into Elanor's room to find her with oxygen tubes in her nose. The sight caught Jenny off guard, but she quickly regained her composure, hoping that she did so before Elanor had a chance to notice her reaction.

"What's that under your arm?" Elanor asked.

"It's a painting," Jenny said sheepishly.

"Let me see." Jenny slowly turned the canvas to show Elanor the painting of the meadow. "That's beautiful. You painted that?"

"Yes ma'am, several years ago."

"Wow. You certainly are talented. That looks like a professional painting!"

"Thank you," Jenny replied. "I was actually thinking it would look nice hanging in here. I noticed you have some empty wall space."

Elanor gasped. "You would like me to have that? Thank you so much. I will love looking at it. It will remind me of you."

Jenny smiled. "Where would you like me to hang it?"

"Oh, don't hang it. Leave it over there." Elanor pointed to the counter by the kitchen area. "This will give me an excuse to call the maintenance man in here. He sure is nice to look at, that one. I'm always looking for reasons to get him in here."

Jenny laughed, and then pretended to be appalled. "Miss Elanor!"

"What? I ain't dead yet."

Jenny placed the painting on the counter and sat in her recliner. "So how are you doing?" she asked in a more serious tone.

Elanor let out a sigh. "Okay. I can't decide what to feel, though. One minute I'm happy that Steve didn't leave me, the next I'm sad because of what happened, then I get angry about it." She fiddled with the tubes in her nose. "I guess you'd call it an emotional roller coaster." Elanor let out a laugh. "But then I get tired and fall asleep. That's an old person's roller coaster."

Keeping Susan's advice in mind, Jenny replied, "I'm about to add a loop-de-loop to your little coaster."

"Oh dear,"

"Do you want to hear it? I don't have to tell you if you'd rather not know."

"No, I'd like to hear it." Elanor sucked in a deep breath. "I just need to tighten my seat belt first."

Jenny recounted the latest vision she'd had, informing Elanor of both Steve's intent to propose and her father's insistence that the marriage never take place. Elanor remained uncharacteristically quiet through the whole story, her expressionless face giving no indication of her mindset. "What are you thinking, Miss Elanor?"

"I'm not sure," she confessed. "I guess I should be happy to know that Steve intended to propose to me. Although, in a way, that makes me sad. I got robbed of the opportunity to spend my life with him."

Jenny made a face.

"What?" Elanor asked.

"Nothing."

"No. Not nothing. You clearly thought of something, now spill it." Elanor's tone was pleasant despite the demanding nature of the words.

Jenny had been raised to always be polite, even if it meant speaking mistruths; with Elanor she knew she needed to speak the truth, even if it meant being impolite. "Well, when I was engaged to my husband, I thought being married to him was going to the most amazing experience in the world. I imagined myself feeling like I'd be walking on air all the time. But the reality of my marriage falls way short of what I'd envisioned." Jenny raised her shoulders to her ears, protecting herself from Elanor's potentially heated response. "It just occurred to me that maybe if you had married Steve, you might have been a little disappointed in how things turned out, too."

Elanor frowned as she considered what Jenny said. "You could be right. I do have this impossible image of what my life would have been like if I got to be with Steve." She let out a snort. "Maybe the real thing *would* have been disappointing."

"Or maybe it wouldn't have," Jenny added. "I don't mean to rain on your parade."

"No, it's not rain; it's reality. A little dose of truth never hurt anyone." Elanor looked kindly at Jenny. "So in what ways do you think your marriage has fallen short?"

Jenny paused for a moment, unable to believe she was about to publicly voice the grievances she'd harbored privately for so long. Saying them out loud would make them real; they would no longer be silly notions she could explain away inside her own head. However, she knew she couldn't live in denial much longer. She and Greg were a ticking time bomb, and an explosion was coming whether she allowed herself to admit it or not.

"It's just not as much of a partnership as I would have hoped," Jenny confessed. "My marriage revolves around his happiness. It's like my role is to make sure everything he desires comes true, even if that means my own wishes get ignored."

"You do realize that can only happen if you let it," Elanor proclaimed casually.

Jenny thought about all of the fights she backed down from, the conversations where she kept her ideas to herself, and the countless concessions she'd made over the years. "You're absolutely right," she admitted. "I have been letting it happen."

"You've got to stand up for yourself, dear. You are important, too—equally as important as your partner. There are no sidekicks in marriages."

A sickening rock formed in Jenny's stomach as she acknowledged she had indeed spent the last seven years being a mere stage hand in the Greg show. Emotion choked Jenny as she quietly confessed, "It's the only role I've ever known."

"Uh oh," Elanor said.

Jenny released some pent-up anxiety with a shaky breath. "I spent my whole life feeling overshadowed by my three older brothers. They were all very promising baseball players, and clearly that was valued in my house. My father would introduce us to people as *my son Brad who plays first base, Tyler who plays short stop and Brandon who pitches. And my daughter Jenny.* That was it. It wasn't *Jenny who paints* or *Jenny who reads two years above grade level.* I was always just Jenny. Jenny who hadn't accomplished anything worth mentioning."

"I can see that in you," Elanor said. "When I look at you I see a lovely young woman with lots of excellent qualities and talents, but I also see a woman who doesn't recognize she has them."

Jenny nodded slowly. Elanor's words had to be true in order for them to sting that much.

"Were your brothers treated special because they were athletes?"

"Oh, yeah," Jenny replied. "Big time. We always had the team back to our house after victories. They were allowed special privileges when they won titles. The house was covered in pictures of them in uniform and framed newspaper clippings with their names highlighted. Every time I finished a painting my father would look at it and say, 'that's nice,' and that was all the reaction I'd get. I'd spend a week on it, and it seemed to only be worth a second of his time. I guess since painting is not a spectator sport and can't earn you a scholarship, he didn't find it to be a worthwhile hobby."

"That's a shame," Elanor commented. "In more ways than one. I think you are amazingly talented, and I wish that would have been fostered for you. You should be proud of your paintings instead of being under-confident in your ability. But not only that, do you realize you went on to marry a man who didn't value your paintings either?" Elanor pointed at the painting on the counter. "*That* should be on display. *That* shouldn't be tucked away because it clashes with furniture. Your husband needs to appreciate how beautiful and special that is. I don't know many people who can make a picture like that."

Jenny silently absorbed Elanor's words. She had nothing to say in return, becoming increasingly aware that even she never recognized the value in herself.

"Don't feel bad about it, dear," Elanor said lightly, as if she were sharing her favorite recipe. "It's the daughter trap. A lot of us fall into it. Little girls often grow up to either marry someone who is just like their father or someone who is the exact opposite. You went for the 'similar' approach. I never got married, but the closest I got was Steve, and he was definitely the opposite of my father. You conformed, I rebelled. We're all guilty of something. It's our baggage."

Jenny hadn't considered the similarities between Greg and her father before, recognizing for the first time the incredible knack both men had for making her feel inadequate. She had spent twenty years trying to earn praise from her father, and then she spent the last six trying to earn it from Greg. That ever-elusive praise seemed to flow freely from Elanor, making Jenny realize she was indeed worthy of it.

Perhaps she had wasted a lifetime seeking affirmation from two men who simply were incapable of giving it.

Jenny lowered her eyebrows in thought and added, "You know, Greg was even an athlete. He played football. I guess I figured if I couldn't *be* the star athlete my father wanted, I could at least bring one home. Maybe then my father would have been proud of me." Jenny could feel her own puzzle pieces clicking into place.

"Did it work?"

"Actually, it did," Jenny said, "for a while, at least. My dad would sit in the stands of the football games when I was in college, cheering and bragging the way he used to do with my brothers. I guess I did feel proud then—like I'd finally accomplished something my father approved of." Jenny looked down at her lap. "Real great way to pick a husband, huh? Choose one that my father would like."

"A lot of us do it." Elanor laughed. "In fact, if women didn't do that, I wouldn't have had a livelihood. The whole focus of my magazine was to make sure women didn't operate on auto-pilot. I wanted them to make conscious choices and not let their baggage call all the shots." Elanor waved her finger at Jenny. "If you had been aware of your issues, you could have made more educated decisions instead of just hopping out of the frying pan into the fire."

Jenny's face reflected the disappointment she felt in herself.

"Like I said, don't feel bad. The sad truth is that when people grow up in a particular environment, they often don't realize there's any other way to do things. You may not have even been aware that it was possible for a man to value what you have to offer." Elanor made a sympathetic face. "Believe it or not, you may have sub-consciously sought out a guy who made you feel inadequate, simply because that was what you were comfortable with. I imagine if a guy came along and treated you like you were an artistic genius, you wouldn't have known what to do with that."

Jenny thought back to a harmless young man named Toby who did, in fact, worship the ground she walked on back in high school. She also thought about how repelled she'd been by him, even though she couldn't pinpoint a specific reason why she'd felt that way. Perhaps his attentiveness had violated her comfort zone. Maybe in her mind, affection was only worth getting if she had to work for it.

Hanging her head, she shifted her focus to the fact that she and Greg shared so few common interests. Leisure days had always meant Jenny agreed to the activity of Greg's choice, even though she would have inevitably selected to do something different if the option had been hers. She began to wonder why that had even been appealing to her. Why hadn't she waited until she found a man who enjoyed the same hobbies that she did? Why had she been so eager to commit to a relationship that required so much compromise on her part? Realizing the mess she had gotten herself into, she placed her head in her hands and declared, "I married my husband for all the wrong reasons."

"If it makes you feel any better, if it wasn't for Steve, I would have done the same thing. I'm sure of it."

Jenny lifted her eyes to Elanor, waiting for elaboration.

"If Steve hadn't fascinated me the way that he did, I guarantee I would have grown up and done everything my parents expected me to. In fact, I was well on that path when Steve showed up at my door. I was banking on meeting a rich boy who may or may not have had a personality, but who had a pedigree I could have been proud of. And a good-looking face, of course. Those were my only requirements until I discovered the importance of character. All I can say is thank God Steve rang my doorbell that day. He saved me from a life of fake smiles and pretentious tea parties."

Although she was happy that Elanor was able to dodge that bullet, Jenny felt overcome with personal regret, wondering exactly where she could have been in life had she made better choices along the way. "I needed to meet Steve," she said softly.

"You did," Elanor reminded her.

"A little too late."

"It's never too late. Look at me. I'm old as hell, and I'm still making discoveries about my life. Shoot, my entire world is getting turned upside down, right here at the end."

Jenny winced. "Yeah, sorry about that."

"Don't be," Elanor said. "I'd rather know the truth." She once again grew distant, clearly bothered by her inability to connect the dots Steve had provided. Shaking her head, she added, "I wish I knew who that gray-haired man was."

Grateful to shift focus away from her own painful self-analysis, Jenny sat up straighter and stated, "Well, he seemed to be the foreman of the construction crew. Do you remember the name of the company Steve worked for?"

Elanor shook her head slowly. "No," she said wistfully, "I wish I did."

A thought popped into Jenny's head. "The real estate records!" she practically shouted.

Her excitement startled Elanor. "What?"

"The real estate records. I don't know why I didn't think of it sooner. It said the name of the builder who constructed the house on Meadowbrook Road." Pulling her phone out of her purse, Jenny looked up the ownership history of the house. "It says here that it was Larrabee and Sons Custom Home Builders. Does that name ring a bell to you?"

Elanor frowned. "Not especially."

"Huh," Jenny said. "Well, at least this gives me something to look into. Maybe this will help me identify the gray-haired man."

"I hope so. And try as I might, I still can't figure out what was meant by Lake Wimsat, either. I've thought about it almost constantly, but I haven't been able to come up with anything."

Jenny smiled. "I think your friend Steve needs to be a little less cryptic and a little more straight-forward."

Elanor looked around the room, shouting "You hear that Steve? Cut the shit and just tell it like it is!"

Both ladies laughed, continuing the conversation for a short while until Elanor started to look tired again. Jenny wished Elanor a good night and headed back to Evansdale, eager to investigate her new lead.

Jenny herself was tired when she got home but was far too curious to go to sleep. Instead she headed for her laptop, looking up the Larrabee and Sons website. She found the site to be elegant, clearly representing a reputable business geared toward wealthier clients. The company name was followed by the slogan *Where*

86

Dreams Become Reality, then in smaller print *family owned and operated since 1926*. Inspired that the site may contain some of the business's history, Jenny read every word on every tab, only to find nothing relevant. She wasn't too disappointed, realizing what a long shot it had been, but she did jot down the phone number with the intent to call in the morning. Perhaps the right person could tell her the information the website did not.

The following morning, Jenny heard the doorbell as she just finished dressing after her shower. Brimming with curiosity she headed downstairs to find Greg standing in the doorway with a woman Jenny didn't recognize. Greg's glance at Jenny demonstrated his displeasure with the guest.

The guest, however, gave Jenny a broad smile. "Ahh, yes," she began. "You must be Jenny."

"Yes ma'am." Jenny tucked her wet hair behind her ear, waiting for an explanation.

"I'm Nancy Carr." The woman held out her hand, which Jenny apprehensively shook. "I'm an interior decorator with Ashley Leavenworth designs. I've been hired by Elanor Whitby to look at some of your paintings and see what furnishings we can find to complement those paintings."

Despite Nancy's generous smile, Jenny stood frozen, her mouth agape. She was aware she should have been saying something, but she wasn't sure what.

Greg broke the silence. "We do appreciate you coming by, but we can't afford new furniture."

"Oh, no, Mr. Watkins," Nancy assured him. "Ms. Whitby will be paying for all of the furniture, and all of my time." Nancy leaned in closer to Greg, placing her hand on his arm and adding through closed teeth, "And she said the sky's the limit." Nancy returned her focus to Jenny. "It seems she's taken quite a liking to you. She said you're like the granddaughter she never had, and she made me promise to treat you like a top priority customer. In fact, I cancelled a pretty important appointment in order to come here today."

Jenny, still at a loss for words, glanced over at Greg who appeared to be quite disapproving of the whole scenario. "We *have* perfectly nice furniture. I don't believe it needs to be replaced yet."

"I'm sure your furniture is lovely," Nancy replied in an overly-chipper tone. "I'm not suggesting there's anything wrong with it. Ms. Whitby just wants to make sure your new furnishings match your wife's paintings so they can be displayed." Still smiling, she glanced back and forth between Jenny and Greg, trying to gauge a reaction. "I've been told I'm not allowed to take no for an answer…"

Jenny bit her lip as the humor of the situation arose within her. "Well, then," she said with stifled laughter. "I guess I should go get my paintings."

After Nancy left, Jenny walked from room to room, trying to envision the new furniture they had just ordered with her paintings serving as a centerpiece. She couldn't help but smile at the thought of people inquiring about the artwork, and her being able to say they were her creations. For the first time since she and Greg moved in together, she was going to feel like the place she called home was half hers.

She ventured downstairs and found Greg sitting on the couch with his laptop, researching kitchen countertops. She slid into the seat next to him and began, "You know, I was thinking we could donate all of our current furniture to a needy family in the area."

"I don't know, babe," Greg replied. "It's really nice stuff, and it's not that old. I'm not sure I'd like to *donate* it. We could probably get some decent money for it if we put an ad in the paper."

Jenny made a face. "I know we could get good money for it, but I was thinking it would be nice if we made somebody else's day the way Elanor just made ours. Pay it forward, you know?"

"Maybe some of it, but not all." Greg took a mental inventory. "The armchair is a little bit worn, so we could probably give that away. And the ottoman with the broken leg. But the rest of the stuff is still really nice…too nice to just give away." Greg turned back to his computer as if the conversation was finished.

Both sadness and shame arose within Jenny. As her husband's true colors rose closer to the surface, she was finding him to be increasingly unattractive. She wondered if those qualities had always been there and she was just too blind to see them until now, or if a new side of Greg was coming out in response to Jenny's rising confidence. She decided it was most likely a mixture of both.

"I'd actually like to discuss this more," Jenny replied uncharacteristically.

Upon hearing her words, Greg closed his computer and turned toward her, but his expression clearly indicated his actions were to appease her.

"See?" Jenny said, "This is what I'm talking about."

"What?"

"I can tell by the look on your face that you're not really going to listen to me. I may get a turn to speak, but at the end of it all you're just going to tell me that we're selling the furniture anyway."

"It just doesn't make any sense to give it away, that's all. Here we are working so hard to renovate this house to make money; why would we want to turn around and give stuff away for free when we could sell it?"

"To be nice," Jenny contended. "To make the world a better place. To help a family in need."

"We are a family in need," Greg replied.

Jenny rolled her eyes at her husband's distorted sense of poverty. "You know, this isn't really about furniture. What upsets me is that whenever we disagree about something, you always assume we're going to do things your way."

"That's not true."

"It most certainly is true."

"Name another time when I did that."

Jenny thought for only a short time before an incident popped into her head. "The kitchen," she said. "I said it should be mustard colored, but you said it should be tan. I assume you're going to insist it be tan."

"Tan is more neutral. Buyers would like it better."

"Neutral doesn't mean colorless. Neutral just means it can go with different decors." Jenny put up her hand to stop herself. "This isn't about paint either. My point is that you always insist on doing everything your way."

"Hey, I'm willing to compromise about the furniture. Didn't I say we could give some of it away?"

"Yeah, the two broken pieces that wouldn't sell anyway. That's real generous of you."

"I don't know what you want from me."

"I want you to listen to me. I want you to respect my opinion."

"Well did you ever stop to think that the reason I don't listen to your opinion is because it never makes sense?"

Jenny closed her eyes and got up from the couch. She headed up the stairs to her bedroom, plopping down on the bed, staring blankly at the ceiling. Had they just crossed the line into a verbally abusive relationship? Potentially. What was she going to do about it?

She had no idea.

She thought about that sweet boy Toby from high school, wondering what he was up to these days. She imagined he was married, possibly with children. She envisioned him coming home from work, scooping up his kids in his arms and greeting them with kisses. She could see him doing the dishes after dinner and asking his wife about her day. She had been such a fool to dismiss him so quickly. What had been the problem? Was he was too nice? Too available? Too doting? "Yeah, such terrible qualities," she snorted as she covered her face with her hands.

The world had been at her fingertips back then, but she didn't have the sense to see it. She had been surrounded by open doors with no ability to determine which ones were worth entering. As she lay in her bed, her body physically ached with the desire to go back in time and do things differently. "Nobody should be allowed to make any decisions until they turn twenty five," she muttered to no one, rolling over onto her side. With a sigh she added, "At least not me."

She settled into the pillow, staring at the wall that would inevitably be painted tan. She felt tired, but not the kind of tired that resulted from a hard day's work. She felt emotionally tired, wanting nothing more than to stay in bed all day and avoid the life she'd created for herself. She didn't want to renovate. She didn't want to face Greg. All she wanted was a time machine so she could go back to high school and strike up a conversation with dear, sweet Toby.

She closed her eyes, riddled with remorse, wondering if this was what depression felt like.

"Arthur Larrabee."

The words were like a splash of cold water on her face. She shot upright, realizing she couldn't lie in bed all day; Elanor was counting on her, as was Steve for that matter. "Arthur Larrabee," she repeated to help her remember. "Arthur Larrabee." She put her feet on the floor and declared, "Snap out of it, Jenny Watkins. Time to get busy."

Jenny arrived at the Larrabee and Sons main office, which was actually a modified model home. She thought about how smart it was to have their headquarters be an example of their handiwork. When she walked through the front door, she looked around the expansive house in awe; they had certainly pulled out all the stops with this floor plan. The house looked like something that could have been featured in a magazine.

A secretary walked out of what would have been a formal living room if the house had been owned by a family. "Hello," she said smiling, "How can I help you today?"

"I have an appointment to meet with Zack Larrabee. My name is Jenny Watkins."

"Okay, Ms. Watkins. I'll let him know you're here. In the meantime, please help yourself to some goodies in the kitchen." The secretary gestured in the direction Jenny should go, and then she disappeared around the corner to go find Zack.

Jenny felt markedly underdressed as her the clacking of her flip flops echoed throughout the museum-like home. She arrived at the kitchen to find a granite kitchen island with a plate of cookies and a bucket of sodas and waters on ice. "Don't mind if I do," she said to herself, cringing when she realized how loudly her voice carried. She made a mental note that she needed to stop talking to herself quite so much.

Just as she took a bite of cookie, a man who looked to be about thirty came into the kitchen. He was wearing a shirt and a tie which looked horribly awkward on him. His unkempt hair and goatee led Jenny to believe he would much rather be rock climbing than pitching custom homes. However, he was polite and professional as he extended his hand. "Zack Larrabee. You must be Jenny Watkins."

Jenny nodded but did not reply; her mouth was full of cookie.

"I know, they're good aren't they? My sister makes them; she's an awesome cook."

Jenny swallowed and said, "Yes, they're delicious."

"Well, feel free to grab a couple more if you'd like."

"No, I'm good," Jenny said, slightly embarrassed.

Zack watched out of the corner of his eye as the secretary resumed her place in her office. He lowered his voice and whispered, "I'm actually going to take one. It's chocolate chip day. That's my favorite." He stealthily took a cookie and snuck a bite. "Mmm. So good."

Jenny couldn't help but smile. While Zack wasn't the best looking guy she'd ever seen, he certainly had an adorable personality.

"If you'll follow me, my office is this way." Zack led Jenny into a room that seemed to be in a library or a study. He took a seat behind a beautiful wooden desk, inviting Jenny to sit in a leather chair reserved for customers. She concluded she was most definitely underdressed.

"So what can I do for you today?"

Jenny let out a sigh. "I actually would like to know a little bit about the history of your company." Jenny looked down at her lap. "I understand if you don't want to waste your time with me considering I won't result in a sale."

Zack leaned back in his chair. "It's a slow day. Actually, summer is my slow season. Everybody wants to move in the summer, so that means everyone is in *here* in October." He pointed to his desk. "Right now the construction guys are overwhelmed, but here in the design center, things are pretty boring. So what would you like to know?"

Jenny sighed again, making a second mental note that she needed to do that less frequently as well. "I was wondering if you could tell me who worked on a property on Meadowbrook Road back in 1954."

"We wouldn't have records going back that far," he explained. "Do you mind telling me what this is about?"

"It's about a murder," Jenny confessed. "One of the members on that crew disappeared one weekend, never to be seen again. The construction site was the last place he was ever seen alive. I was wondering if you could track down some of his coworkers so I could ask if they know anything about it."

Zack seemed genuinely interested. "Murder, huh? That's pretty heavy stuff. I'd certainly love to help out if I can." He made a face. "Like I said, we don't have those kinds of records just lying around, but I could potentially do some digging for you."

"That'd be great."

"Are you a detective?" Zack asked.

"No." Jenny shook her head.

"Was the murdered guy a relative of yours?"

Again Jenny shook her head. She could see Zack's confusion, so she decided to go out on a limb. "I'm a psychic."

"No way," Zack said dumbfounded.

Jenny smiled sheepishly, nodding in affirmation.

"That is so cool. I totally believe in that stuff. So..." Zack seemed unsure of what to ask, even though he obviously had a million questions.

Jenny decided to put him out of his misery. "I moved here recently, and I started hearing voices in my new house. You probably know the house, actually. It sticks out like a sore thumb. It's that really big house on Autumn Drive."

Zack lit up like a child. "That's one of our houses!"

"Really?"

"No lie. That house kept our business from going under way back when. In fact, we used to show it to people before..." Zack stopped suddenly, clearly becoming aware that his next words could be offensive to the home's new owner.

"Before it went to hell? Is that what you were going to say?"

Zack blushed and smiled, showing every one of his teeth. "Something to that effect."

"Well, I'm certainly not offended. We bought the house dirt cheap to flip it. We're hoping to make it look the way it did when your company first built it." For a brief moment Jenny regretted disclosing that she was a member of a 'we.'

"It would be great if you could do that."

"It's worth a shot," Jenny said. "Anyway, once I moved in I heard a voice saying two names. The first name was Steve O'dell, the missing man, and the second was Elanor Whitby."

"The Whitbys lived in that house for decades."

"I know. I was able to figure that out with some research. I hired a private investigator to help me find Elanor, and she told me that Steve had been her boyfriend back in 1954. One weekend he disappeared and she never saw him again. He was working for your company at the time, more specifically at that house on Meadowbrook Road. That's why I'd like to see who was on the crew—to see if anyone knows anything."

"How do you know he was murdered?"

Jenny felt slightly foolish as she disclosed, "I saw it in a vision."

93

"You *saw* it?"

"Actually," Jenny interlaced her fingers and placed them on his desk. "I felt it. I had the vision through the victim's eyes, and I experienced him getting shot."

"Whoa." Zack sat up straight in his chair. "That's crazy."

"Tell me about it."

"So did you see who killed him?"

"I did, so I know what he looks like," Jenny confessed, "but I don't know who he was. I do know it happened at the construction site on a Saturday morning. Steve was lured there by a coworker— presumably the foreman—who shot him from behind."

"What did he look like? The killer, I mean."

"He was an older guy, with gray hair. The sad thing is, he's got to be dead by now. If he had gray hair back in 1954, there's no way he'd still be alive today. We'll never be able to get justice for Steve, but even still I would like to give Elanor some answers. She's dying of cancer, and all she'd like to know is who was responsible for her boyfriend's death. And why."

Zack slapped his hand on his desk. "Well, then, let's get her some answers."

Jenny was grateful for his enthusiasm, but saddened that similar zeal couldn't come from her own husband. Was she married to the only person in the world who didn't find her ability to be fascinating?

"Okay," Jenny said sighing, "Let's think about this." Something clicked in her head. "Wait a minute. You said the house on Autumn Drive was a Larrabee home, right?"

"Yup."

"And it kept your company from going out of business?"

"That's the story."

Jenny started to do some quick math in her head. The business had been family owned and operated since 1926. The house had been built in 1933. The man who had been in charge of building that house must have had gray hair by 1954, and he'd be indebted to Elanor's father for saving his business. Suddenly the pieces were clicking into place.

"Who founded this company, do you know?" Jenny asked.

"My great-grandfather, Arthur Larrabee."

Jenny froze. "I've actually heard his name in a message. Do you have a picture of him, by any chance?"

"Not lying around, but I'm sure I could dig one up. If I don't have one, my father will." Zack gave Jenny a strange look. "Why, do you think he was the shooter?"

"Would it offend you if I said yes?"

"No. Would it disturb you if I told you I think it'd be cool to have a murderer in the family?"

Jenny laughed. "No."

"Okay, then we're good." Zack looked somewhat puzzled. "My only question is what motive he would have had."

"Debt."

"Debt?"

"I imagine he felt like he owed Elanor's father something for saving his business. Elanor's father despised Steve and wanted him gone. I'm thinking your great-grandfather pulled the trigger to repay a debt to an old friend."

"Who knew my family history was so juicy?" Zack marveled. "I always thought they were just boring old people, but they've got some serious skeletons in their closets, huh?"

"It appears so."

"I'll tell you what. After you leave, I'll start doing some investigating. Make some phone calls. I'll get back to you if I find anything. Do you mind if I have your phone number?"

"Not at all," Jenny said. She gave Zack the number, and he programmed it into his phone.

"I'll text you with my number. That way you can call me directly if you need me for anything, and you don't have to pretend to want to buy a home in order to talk to me." Another toothy grin.

"Sounds great. Thank you for being so helpful. I wasn't quite sure what to expect when I came here. I was afraid you'd slam the door in my face."

"A few of my cousins probably would have. They're all business. If you're not here to buy a home, then don't waste their time." Zack stood up. "Larrabees come with varying degrees of stuffiness."

Jenny followed suit and stood up as well. "I'm glad I got the laid back one, then."

"I'm glad you got me too." Zack giggled like a little girl. "This is so cool."

Zack walked Jenny out to the door, sneaking another cookie from the kitchen as he walked by. "I'll get on this right away," he said. "You've just made my boring life very exciting."

"Boring life?" Jenny remarked before she had the chance to stop herself. "I doubt that."

"My life consists of work, frozen dinners and…work. That's not exactly thrilling."

"My home life consists of patching drywall and scraping wallpaper," Jenny rebutted. "You want to trade?"

Zack pretended to think for a moment. "Umm…no. I did enough of that stuff as a teenager. I didn't always have this prestigious desk job, you know." He smoothed his tie and displayed a cheesy smile. "I spent a lot of years out there in the trenches, swinging a hammer. I've had enough of that to last a lifetime."

"Me too, and I've only been doing it two weeks."

With a laugh and a quick goodbye, Jenny made her exit. As she walked to her car, she felt positively exhilarated. Zack was definitely endearing in an opposite-of-Greg kind of way. This was the first time a guy had peaked her interest in a long time. Although she was fully aware she couldn't have him for herself, she had to admit she was happy about Zack's life of obvious bachelorhood. She would have been disappointed if he had been taken. Was that selfish of her? Maybe. But human nature was ugly sometimes.

More importantly, however, she was delighted to finally have answers for Elanor. While she didn't have proof, the dates seemed to match up. The motive was reasonable. That had to be how things unfolded. Now it made sense that Steve's visions implicated both a gray-haired man and her father. They were both to blame.

Nothing, not even the grief Greg would inevitably dish out when she got home, could bring Jenny down from her high.

Chapter 12

Jenny walked through the doorway, immediately noticing her painting hanging on the wall adjacent to the television. She smiled and glanced at Elanor, making sure she was awake. "It looks nice."

"It sure does. Do you think it looks good there?"

"I think it looks great there."

"I could have it moved if you think it would look better over there." Elanor pointed to the opposite wall. "Believe me, I don't mind having the handyman come back in."

Jenny laughed. "It looks great where it is, but it would look fine over there, too, if you'd like him to pay you another visit." Jenny sat down in her chair. "Speaking of visits...we had a very interesting guest of our own the other day."

"Oh?" Elanor asked coyly. "And who might that have been?"

"Just a wonderful woman named Nancy Carr who bought tons and tons of beautiful furniture for us."

"Oh, good." Elanor said more seriously. "I'm glad she came. I've worked with Nancy for years. She's a sweet woman, isn't she?"

"Yes ma'am. And so is the woman who sent her."

Elanor shooed away Jenny's compliment with her hand. "Nancy does good work. I've always been impressed by her. She helped me decorate my entire house at the lake, several times over. I don't really have a knack for that kind of thing, and she was a real life saver. I hope you found her to be helpful."

"You have no idea," Jenny said. "She could walk into a room and tell us exactly what it needed. She was amazing."

"I know. She's fabulous." Elanor clasped her hands together excitedly. "So tell me what furniture you got."

"Wow. Where to begin," Jenny stated. "We got a new family room set to replace the one we had—that will match a painting I made of a mountain scene--and we got new bedding to match a river painting I'd done. Then we bought furniture to fill the rooms that were previously empty. We came from an apartment, so we didn't have too much. Now we have a house full of beautiful furniture, thanks to you." Jenny felt a little guilty. "We even replaced our kitchen set, not to match any of my paintings, but because the decorator said our modern set looked out of place in a historic home. I hope you don't mind."

"Mind? Of course I don't mind. I sent her over there, didn't I?"

Jenny giggled. "Yes, I suppose you did. And I can't thank you enough. That was really generous of you."

"Aw, it was nothing. With all that you've done for me, it was the least I could do. You're helping me unravel the mystery of what happened to Steve. That's worth more than a little bit of furniture."

"Well," Jenny said, patting Elanor on the leg. "You may really be getting your money's worth. I just may have the answer we've been looking for."

Elanor's face went white. "What did you find out?"

"Arthur Larrabee, the founder of Larrabee and Sons Custom Homes, actually built the house you grew up in. Your father saved him from bankruptcy, so maybe he returned the favor by doing your father's dirty work. I'm thinking Arthur Larrabee was that gray-haired man from my vision. He apparently started his business in 1926, so by the time the house on Meadowbrook Road was built in 1954, he very easily could have had gray hair. And we know Larrabee and Sons was the company that Steve was working for, so it fits."

Elanor silently contemplated Jenny's words for quite some time. "That makes sense," she eventually said. "That makes perfect sense." She turned to Jenny. "Do you have any way of knowing for sure that it was him?"

"One of the younger Larrabees is going to look for a picture of Arthur for me. I'll be able to tell if he was the same man from my vision."

"I'm sure it will be. It has to be." Elanor sank back into her bed, looking more relaxed than she had in a while. "I finally got my answers. After all these years, now I know what happened." She released a deep breath. "Now I can die peacefully."

"Slow down there, sister. You don't need to go passing away on me just because you have your answer."

Still reclined against her pillow, Elanor smiled kindly and replied, "You're the only one who will miss me, you know."

"That can't be true," Jenny said sincerely.

Elanor looked distant. "Oh, it's true." She raised her eyes to meet Jenny's. "I never married. I had no kids. I have no siblings. No nieces. No nephews. And I was a little too much of a corporate bitch to have any true friends. When you're in charge of a company, you have to keep people at arm's length. I was nice to people and all, but I didn't really pal around with any of my staff outside of work. I didn't want to be accused of playing favorites at promotion time. I also needed to make sure I could let people go if necessary. You don't want to have to be in the position of firing one of your friends. Making personal relationships at work only gets messy when you're the boss."

"I get that," Jenny stated. "But honestly, it surprises me that you never married. You're such a hoot. I would have thought that men would be pounding down your door."

"A couple did," Elanor confessed. "But the truth was I was married to my job. I was only leading them on by acting like I wanted a relationship." Elanor looked solemn. "I hurt two very nice boys when I was younger. I still feel bad about that."

"Do you feel like talking about it?" Jenny asked.

"They're long stories."

"I've got time," Jenny said. "I'm trying to avoid going home, remember?"

Elanor let out a laugh. "Gosh. Let me see how much I can remember. I haven't thought about those boys in ages.

"The first was a young man named Ronald; he worked with me at the grocery store right after I moved out of my parents' house. He was a dear, sweet thing. Very innocent. And boy was he ever good looking. My, oh, my. He was right up there with Marlon Brando and Paul Newman."

Jenny had to smirk at the dated references, but even she had to admit that very few men rivaled a young Paul Newman.

"Needless to say every girl who worked at that store was smitten with him. Every girl but me, that is. I was still holding out hope that Steve was coming back at that point, so I had no interest in boys, no matter how good-looking they were. While every other girl in the store was busy tripping over herself to be noticed by Ronald, I treated him like anyone else. I think that made me stand out in his eyes, so he actually became quite smitten with me. I was the only woman in the store who posed a challenge to him. It's funny…people always seem to want what they can't have.

"Anyway, he asked me out several times, and I always declined. I never gave him a reason; I just said no. But he kept asking. His persistence eventually paid off, too, because I finally caved.

"Actually, I only agreed to go out with him out of rebellion. After about a year, I started to accept that Steve wasn't coming back, and at that point I became angry. I kind of thought to myself, 'screw him,' and I agreed to go out with Ronald. There's no better way to get back at a guy than going out with someone who looks like a movie star, right?"

Jenny had to grin. "Good point."

"I do feel a little bit bad about the whole thing, even to this day. My motives weren't really that great; I never did have any serious feelings for Ronald. He was so kind, and he treated me so well, but he wasn't very bright. Or ambitious. He worked at the grocery store for a while, and eventually he earned the title of assistant frozen food manager. He was so proud. It was step one of his goal, which was eventually being *the* frozen food manager." Elanor shook her head. "Maybe I'm a snob, but I could never settle down with a guy whose only goal was to be a worker bee in a grocery store. Not when I was on a mission to change the world.

"But he served a purpose in my life at the time. He was *someone*. Having him in my life meant I wasn't sitting around waiting anymore. It meant I was taking some control of my life back." Elanor got a mischievous smile on her face. "And it didn't hurt that he was so good looking. Man. He was just about the best distraction any girl could have asked for."

Jenny giggled. Even though she knew Elanor quite well at that point, something was still very strange about an elderly woman talking about how hot a guy was.

"But he was fun," Elanor said kindly, returning to her story. "He truly was. He was simple, but we did have some good times together." She let out a sigh. "I ended up hurting that poor boy. I didn't mean to, but I did. While I was just having some fun, he was busy falling in love with me. It never ends nicely when the love is one-sided."

"Uh-oh," Jenny said, "What happened?"

"He proposed," Elanor said with sadness. "And I had to say no. I felt positively awful about it at the time, but you know…I have thought about it since then, and I realize I wasn't entirely to blame. You can't fall in love with a free-spirited woman and then become angry when she won't settle down with you. I made no secret of the fact that I was out to change the world, but when Ronald looked into the future he saw me being nothing more than a wife and baby machine. If his view of the future didn't come true, it's only because he had a very unrealistic view of the future."

"Even I know you wouldn't have agreed to that, and I just met you," Jenny said.

"Exactly," replied Elanor. "I think he just figured if I was in love with him enough, I'd be willing to abandon my dreams and settle down." She shook her head. "But he was young, too. I imagine he just didn't know any better back then. I'm hoping he took that as a learning experience and realized that if he wanted a woman who would marry him and have babies, he'd need to find a woman who wanted to get married and have babies." She looked a little sad. "I'm hoping that's how he looks at it, anyway. I hope he didn't harbor hatred and resentment toward me all these years."

"Probably not," Jenny said reassuringly. "I imagine he went on to find a woman who fit better into his life. Once he met her, he probably realized that you two weren't really a good match." Jenny shrugged. "In fact, if he ultimately ended up happy, he may have been grateful that you turned him down. When push came to shove, he didn't really want to be married to you. He wanted to be married to a more…" Jenny searched for the correct word, "traditional woman."

"Oh, I know that," Elanor said. "I just wonder if *he* knows it. Like I said, he wasn't very bright. But he was good looking. Did I mention that?" The evil smile returned.

"Once or twice," Jenny replied giggling.

"I wish I had a picture of him," Elanor said. "You'd be impressed."

"I'm sure I would be."

"You know, though," Elanor said, scratching her head. "I do have to wonder...He seemed sweet and innocent and all, but sometimes I think he was a little more selfish than I give him credit for."

"What makes you say that?"

"The timing," Elanor stated. "He proposed to me right at the moment my magazine was taking off. It's as if he sensed he was losing me, so he wanted to...trap me. Make me his. You know? I'd like to think that if he truly loved me, he would have been happy for me that my dream was coming true. But he certainly was *not* happy for me when I was becoming successful. I believe my success threatened him. I think he wanted to keep me small so that I wouldn't outgrow him. Either that, or he wanted to be the star of the show. He wanted it to be *grocery store manager Ronald Dwyer and his wife Elanor,* not *magazine mogul Elanor and her husband Ronald.*"

A rock formed in the pit of Jenny's stomach as a wave of unpleasant familiarity overcame her.

Not sensing Jenny's mood shift, Elanor continued. "I guess I'll never know for sure what he was thinking, but if either of my suspicions are correct, those are ugly traits."

"I agree," Jenny said softly. "I definitely agree."

"I know you do," Elanor said. "It's one of the reasons I could recognize your situation. I lived it. I see a lot of similarity between Ronald and your husband. They both wanted their flags to look higher by keeping ours low, and that's not the way it should be."

"Nope. It sure isn't." Jenny said, although she was mostly talking to herself. Eager to change the subject, Jenny added, "What about the other guy? You said there were two."

Elanor rubbed her eyes, which were starting to show signs of fatigue. "The other gentleman was a young man named Mike who couldn't have been more different than Ronald. I met Mike, oh, I don't know, I guess when I was twenty seven or twenty eight. It was a few years after Ronald. My magazine was in full swing by then, and Mike was a graphic designer. I had hired him as a contractor; he did good work."

"Is that all you can say about him? He was a contractor who did good work?"

This time Elanor laughed. "No, there was more to it than that. Definitely. Not at first, though. In the beginning we had a strictly professional relationship. He was as much of a workaholic as I was, and I daresay he was even more of a perfectionist. We spent many nights working late, trying to get the magazine layout to look just so. Naturally we took breaks from time to time and talked about more personal matters. It turned out we had a good deal in common."

"Oh really," Jenny said curiously.

"Yes, really," Elanor said in the same tone. "He had very similar views to me and Steve, actually. He was very progressive, which explained why he took the job at my magazine. He liked the message my magazine sent. I didn't offer him the most money, as it turned out, but he wasn't all about money. He was a man of great principle. That is, of course, until the night he planted a kiss on me in the office." Elanor laughed. "It caught me off guard, to say the least."

"Oh?"

"We were sitting very close together, eyeing the same page, trying to decide how the layout should be. We glanced at each other— our eyes met—and he kissed me as if consumed with passion. It was like he couldn't help himself." She made a guilty face. "He clearly thought the feeling was mutual, but it wasn't. I think since he felt it so strongly, he thought I had to feel it, too. But, of course, I'm a woman made of stone, and I only regarded him as a cherished friend and coworker at the time."

"You're not made of stone," Jenny said.

"Sometimes I wonder," Elanor stated. "How else could I have gone through life without loving anybody but Steve? Honestly, if I was going to love anyone else, it should have been Mike. There was no reason I shouldn't have loved him. He was everything I could have asked for. I even knew that at the time, so I decided to accept his advances, even though I didn't have any romantic feelings for him. I thought maybe I had just been so career-oriented for so long that I'd shut off that part of my life. Perhaps if I allowed someone in, I would rediscover my romantic side, so to speak, and I'd feel love again. I *wanted* to feel love again. I remembered how wonderful it felt to be with Steve. If I could have recaptured that with another man, I would have been on top of the world. And Mike seemed like as good a candidate as any.

"So we dated. We dated for a long time, but try as I might, I never did feel anything for him. I went through the motions, but you can't create feelings that just aren't there. And sadly, they just weren't there."

"So I assume you eventually ended it?" Jenny asked.

"Yes, I did," Elanor said nodding. "I ended it before he had a chance to propose. I had learned my lesson from Ronald not to let it go that far."

"How did he take it?"

"Quite well, actually," Elanor said, "just as I suspected he would. He was independent enough that a break up wouldn't have devastated him. But he was hurt, I can't lie." She looked a little sad. "At first he tried to stay on board as my graphic designer, but after a while he decided it was too difficult to work with me without being in my life. He quit a short time later."

"Did you stay in touch with him?"

"Somewhat, yes," Elanor said. "I know he did go on to eventually get married. I'm not sure if he ever had kids or not. But I do think he ultimately was happy, which made me happy. I genuinely liked the man; I just couldn't bring myself to love him."

"So how old were you when it ended?"

Elanor let out a deep breath as she did a little math in her head. "Oh, I don't know. Thirty? Thirty-one? Somewhere around there."

"And those were the only two men in your life?"

"After that I gave up. I was only hurting people." Elanor made a face. "You know, it was easier than it should have been for me to shut off that part of my life. You would think I would have been lonely, but I wasn't. That's why I wonder if something was wrong with me. Most women want to have someone in their lives. I was happy with just a magazine." She looked at Jenny. "That doesn't seem normal."

A strange wave washed over Jenny. Unsure of what it meant, she remained quiet about it.

"Everybody's different," Jenny said. "I actually think it's pretty cool that you didn't feel the need to have a man by your side.

I'm sure it made your life a lot less complicated." Jenny snorted. "In fact, I'm jealous. Right now being single seems quite appealing."

"You know, it wasn't a bad thing. Not to me, anyway. Some people judged me because of it, but you know I don't give a shit about that." Elanor squinted in thought. "It's funny…if a man decides to forego a family in favor of a business, he's considered to be ambitious. Or maybe he's just such an eligible bachelor that he can't bring himself to settle down with only one gorgeous woman. But if a woman opts for a career instead of a family, people assume she's cold, or she's too demanding for any man to tolerate her. It's like people can't wrap their heads around a woman purposely dedicating her life to her job."

"You know, you're right. There is that double standard." Jenny had actually been guilty of it herself in the past.

"Believe me, I felt it. Sometimes when women would talk about their families in a crowd, they would catch my eye and suddenly become quiet. It's as if they assumed I must have wanted that life but never got it, and talking about it in front of me was cruel. I never felt any pangs of longing when I heard about other peoples' families. That was their path. The magazine was mine." She shrugged. "It's as simple as that.

"The only time I felt any type of regret was when I first retired from the magazine. I only retired because my health had reached the point where I couldn't handle it anymore, so I wasn't in any condition to do any serious traveling or anything. Besides, I had no one to travel with. I spent a lot of time sitting around my house at first, and while I loved it there, I found myself feeling like a caged animal. Keep in mind I had once been a very busy woman. I'd easily put in fourteen, sixteen hour days, six days a week and still feel like I hadn't accomplished everything I needed to do. People always needed me to be in three different places at once. For decades my life was absolutely crazy, and I loved every minute of it.

"But then I suddenly found myself with nothing to do. No place to be. Nobody needed me. The despair I felt took my breath away. That's why I ended up selling the house and coming here. I wanted to be with people, and not just the ones I hired to take care of me. I wanted friends. And at first it was great, but after a while a lot of the friends I made started dying. It was very depressing. And then my health reached the point where it was difficult to go out into the common area anymore. Now I just spend a lot of my time in here. Waiting to die." She looked at Jenny. "And waiting for your visits."

Jenny's heart ached as she realized she was being selfish for wanting Elanor to live longer. She hadn't considered what the hours were like for Elanor when they weren't together. Long and lonely. While Jenny found herself overwhelmed with too much to do, Elanor had nothing to occupy her time. At that moment Jenny's perspective changed, and she had a little more sympathy for Elanor's plight.

"I do hope you don't stop visiting now that the mystery's solved," Elanor added.

"Of course I won't," Jenny proclaimed. "I love our visits. Besides, the story isn't *entirely* clear. We still haven't figured out what Lake Wimsat meant."

"Maybe he was just referring to the good times we had there," Elanor said sleepily.

"Or maybe there's more he wants us to know..."

Chapter 13

"Do you want to drive or do you want me to?" Jenny posed, throwing her purse strap over her shoulder.

"If you could drive, that'd be great." Greg replied. "I'd like to spend some more time looking through the catalogs. I wanted to be a little better prepared than this, but time just got away from me. I would like to have an idea of what I want instead of just going in there saying, *show me all your cabinets.*"

"Okay, that's fine. So where is the place?" Greg gave Jenny the address, which she typed in her phone. They climbed into the car and headed to the cabinet retailer.

The car ride was silent except for the occasional instructions from the mechanical voice on the phone. Greg thumbed through the pages of the magazine as Jenny absent-mindedly followed the automated directions. She made a turn, and Greg posed, "What are you doing?"

Jenny didn't reply. "You were supposed to turn left. Why did you go right?"

"Shhh." Jenny said to him. She was picking up a vibe that she didn't want to lose.

The voice on the phone squawked repeated commands, which Jenny found distracting. She quickly turned off the phone and placed it on her lap.

"What are you doing?" Greg demanded again.

Jenny waved away his question with her hand. She needed to maintain her concentration.

"Jenny! Where the hell are you going?"

"I need you to be quiet. I'm on to something."

"You're on to something? We have an appointment at the cabinet place. We're going to be late. Now turn on your damn phone and…"

Jenny slammed on the brakes, stopping the car in the middle of the road. "I told you to be quiet. Either stop talking, or get out of the car."

"You've lost your fucking mind."

"Which is it? Are you going to be quiet, or are you going to start walking?"

Greg seethed, but remained quiet while doing so, so Jenny started the car again. She was able to follow the unknown but predetermined path which ultimately led her directly into a park that she had never been to before.

Once inside the park, she followed the windy main road until she knew to take a right down a side street. A short distance down she arrived at the end of the road where a few small parking spaces were carved out. A building sat to her left, demarked with the sign "Facilities Maintenance Building." She knew this was her destination.

Greg started speaking again as she turned off the car. "You're stopping *here*?"

Jenny handed him the keys. "Here. Go on to the cabinet place." She threw her phone into her purse and climbed out of the car.

Greg followed her. "I'm not going without you. I can't just leave you here."

"I'll be fine." Jenny tried to keep her comments short as not to lose her signal.

"We have an appointment. Now get in this car."

Jenny walked toward the edge of the parking lot, staring into the trees. She knew what she was looking for was in those trees.

"Jenny, get in the damn car."

"Go without me," she said half-heartedly.

"Jenny Watkins, I said to get in the damn car."

Jenny turned around and shouted at Greg with a fury she had never exhibited toward anyone. "And I said to go without me! I don't give a shit about the cabinets! They're fucking cabinets; just pick something! I'm dealing with something much more important here.

No go away because you're distracting me." She turned back around to face the trees.

Without another word Greg got into the driver's side of the car, slammed the door, and peeled out of the parking lot. The commotion caused a worker to emerge from the building, looking remarkably unconcerned for Jenny. "Are you okay, ma'am?" he asked half-heartedly.

"Yeah, I'm fine," she replied. "I just married an asshole." She pointed toward the overgrown woods. "Do you mind if I go back here?"

The worker scanned his eyes down Jenny's bare legs, stopping at her flip-flops. Without exhibiting any expression, he shrugged and replied, "If you want."

"Thanks." Jenny turned toward the woods again as the worker went back into the building. "Okay, Steve," She muttered under her breath. "Lead the way."

She trampled through the brush, some of which felt itchy, some of which felt sharp as knives. Bugs encircled her head, but much like a predator tracking a scent, she was oblivious to the distracters. She eventually reached a bit of a clearing that had apparently served as a dumping ground decades earlier. Two rusted service vehicles sat covered with vines, large pieces of scrap metal lay strewn about, as did old wooden beams with nails sticking out of them. Large coils of unused chicken wire were stacked off to the side, loosely masking three fifty-five gallon drums lined neatly in a row.

She stood for a moment, staring at the drums, painfully aware of what she believed she was looking at, hoping she was wrong. She turned around and went back out into the parking lot, heading straight inside the facilities maintenance building. The same worker was there behind a desk, and he looked up at her with a bit of a dismayed expression. Dripping with sweat and covered with bug bites and scratches, Jenny knew she must have looked like a crazy woman.

"Hi," she began, "I know this is a strange question, but those drums back there…Do you know how long they've been there?"

The worker shrugged. "I didn't even know there were drums back there."

"There's a whole mess of junk in the woods. Do you mind if I look through it?"

"Knock yourself out."

"Thanks." Jenny walked back into the oppressive Georgia heat and turned her cell phone back on. She dialed Susan's number, desperately hopeful that she'd be available. Fortunately, Susan answered.

"Hello, Jenny," Susan said. "To what do I owe the pleasure?"

"Hi Susan. I'm sorry to bother you. I really am. But I have found something...I think." Jenny realized she should have rehearsed this phone call before she made it. "I don't know. I'm just not sure what I'm supposed to do."

Susan's tone indicated understanding. "Okay, tell me where you are and I'll be there in a bit."

Jenny sighed with relief. "I'm at the facilities maintenance building at Lake Wimsat State Park. Actually, what I found is behind the building, out into the woods a little ways. You should wear pants and sneakers or boots or something."

"Ahh," Susan said knowingly. "I keep a pair of boots in my car. You'll learn to do the same after a while. Do you need a pair for yourself?"

"That would be great. Do you have a size seven?"

"No, but I have a nine. Better too big than too small."

"Thanks, Susan. You're a life-saver."

"Okay, I'll be out there soon."

Overwhelmed by the heat, Jenny found the embarrassment of facing the maintenance worker to be preferable to waiting outside. She went back into the building, smiled at the worker, and commented, "I'm just going to wait in here for my friend."

He looked expressionlessly at Jenny. "Okay." He clearly couldn't have cared much less.

After what seemed like an uncomfortable eternity, Susan's car pulled into the parking lot. Jenny's pulse quickened as she walked outside to greet Susan, who was opening the back door of her car. Out popped Buddy who, upon seeing Jenny, broke into an excited trot to come say hello. The sight of the dog immediately calmed Jenny's nerves as she knelt down to the ground to greet him.

"Well, hello, Buddy," Jenny said as the dog furiously licked her chin. She talked in a tone often reserved for babies, rubbing Buddy's ears furiously. "Yes, you are a vicious guard dog, aren't you Buddy?"

Susan laughed. "Yeah, right." As Jenny stood up, Susan asked, "So what did you find?" She handed Jenny the boots.

"I'm not entirely sure." Jenny plopped the boots on the ground and wriggled her feet inside them.

"Well, what is it?"

"Let me show you," Jenny said, leading Susan through the tangles of growth behind the building. Buddy showed little desire to attempt the hike, so Susan tucked him under her arm and carried him.

After a few minutes, the ladies arrived back at the dumping ground, and Jenny gestured toward the three drums. "This is it," Jenny said. "For some reason I was led here. I don't even want to tell you what I suspect might be inside."

Susan repositioned the dog under her arm. "Yeah, this may not be good."

Nerves took over Jenny, and words started spewing out of her mouth. "Well, what do we do? Do we open them? What if we find something? How will I explain that I was drawn here by a man who's been dead for sixty years…"

Susan put her hand on Jenny's shoulder. "Relax," she said quickly. "It's okay. I have a friend on the police force who has used my services many times. I can call him and explain that you were led here, and we'd like him to come out and check out the drums. It could be something, it could be nothing…either way, it's okay."

Jenny let out a long breath, releasing a good deal of anxiety along with it. Susan's calm demeanor was incredibly helpful. "That's great. Thank you."

Susan pulled her phone out of her pocket and pressed a button. Jenny noticed the number was on speed dial. After a pause, Susan said, "Hi, Bill, how are you?...Great. The kids doing okay?...Glad to hear that. Yeah, we're doing well. I just saw Jake at college last weekend. We had a nice visit."

Jenny marveled at how nonchalant Susan was considering the circumstances.

"Well, I have made a friend here who is also psychic, and she's discovered something we'd like you to check out…There are a few fifty five gallon drums behind the facilities building at Lake Wimsat State Park…Yeah, a man went missing sixty years ago… Great. We'll see you in a few. Bye." She hung up the phone. "Bill is on his way."

111

Jenny was quite impressed. "I didn't realize you had inside connections at the police force."

Susan laughed. "You're just lucky that I've done the dirty work for you there. Do you know how many police men laughed at me when I called them and told them I was a medium with valuable information? It seems every week they get at least a dozen calls from people claiming the same thing. Most cops just pretty much hung up on me."

"So how did you stumble across this guy?"

"He responded when I found a gun that was used in a murder. When he asked me how I found it, I told him I had dreamt about it. Considering it was down inside a sewer where you'd only be able to find it by lifting up the man-hole cover, he realized I didn't just *happen to* see it. I had to have known where to look." Susan scratched Buddy's head. "That gun was the key piece of evidence they needed to put their guy away. Bill was eternally grateful."

"So does he use you regularly?"

Susan shrugged with her free shoulder. "Sometimes. I'll call him if I have some insight, and a few times he's asked me to look into some of his trickier cases for him. I've been able to help solve a few crimes, or at least provide the guys with the extra boost they need to get the investigation rolling."

"So now do all of the people on the force believe in you?"

"I think most do at this point. There will always be a few who don't, and won't, under any circumstance. I'm not worried about trying to convince them. I'm more concerned with providing people with answers." She turned her attention toward Buddy. "Seriously, dog. You need to get down. You weigh too much to be carried like this." Susan plopped the dog down into the thick brush, clearly to the dog's dismay. He looked up at Susan with sad eyes, wagging his tail slowly.

"So, what do you think is going to happen when Bill gets here?"

"I imagine he'll take a peek inside the drums."

"What if it's what I think it is?"

"Then it stops being your concern and becomes a police matter."

Jenny let out a nervous sigh. She wasn't sure whether she wanted to be right or wrong about what was inside. She'd feel foolish if she were wrong, but she didn't want to have to witness the unveiling of the contents if she were right, either.

"You know," Susan began, "we don't have to stand back here. In fact, we shouldn't. Let's go back to the car so we can flag down Bill when he arrives." She directed her attention to the dog again, "Come on, Buddy-Boo. Up you go." She bent down and scooped Buddy back under her arm and proceeded back to the parking lot.

Once they got back to the parking lot, Susan turned to Jenny and quizzically asked, "How did you get here?"

Jenny had almost forgotten. "Oh. Yeah. I drove here with my husband, but he left."

"He left?"

"He had an appointment."

"Come on. Let's get in the car. It's hotter than hell out here," Susan declared. The ladies got into the car where Susan blasted the air conditioning. Buddy sat in the front seat this time, pressing his nose squarely against the vent, feeling a blast so powerful his ears blew backward. "So your husband just left you here?"

Jenny sighed, unsure how much she wanted to disclose. "Well, I told him to leave. It was kind of ugly. We were both on our way to an appointment, and I was driving. I drove here instead of where we were supposed to go. He wasn't happy about it."

"Ah. I get it," Susan said. "I've lost more than one friend that way. It takes a special kind of person to recognize, and accept, that all the plans they make with you are tentative. Some people just can't stand the idea of their schedule getting constantly changed at the last minute."

"But your husband is okay with it?"

"Yeah, but I think I told you, I already knew I was psychic when I met him. He knew what he was getting into. I usually call him and let him know if I have to cancel our plans or something, and he's fine with it. A few times I haven't been able to call. Some of the locations I end up in are so remote that there's no cell phone service. But he understands that. He operates under the assumption that if I don't show up somewhere, I'm busy working. I'm very lucky that way."

"But you have lost some friends?"

"Yes, some. But most people are okay with it. They understand I'm not just forgetting to hang out with them, or I haven't decided I'd rather do something else." Susan laughed. "It actually helps that most of my friends are moms." She turned to Jenny. "Do you have kids?"

"No, not yet."

"Well, when you do, you'll realize that every plan you make is tentative when you have babies. You can be on your way out the door with the baby on your hip, and suddenly the kid pukes everywhere. Either that, or the morning nap lasts for four hours, so you have to skip your lunch date with your friend. It just goes without saying among young moms that you can't always deliver on your promises, and you can't always call to cancel, either. Most of my friends understand that, and they aren't upset with me when I don't show up places. They've come to expect it."

Jenny nodded, contemplating how wonderful it would have been for Greg to be that understanding. Once again a wave of regret washed over her; she wondered how different her life would have looked if she had done something as simple as sign up for a different World History class.

In an attempt to keep the conversation light, Jenny asked, "So, how many kids do you have?"

"Three. Two sons and a daughter. My oldest, Jake, is a junior in college. My middle son, Kevin, is a senior in high school, and my daughter Christine is a sophomore in high school."

"I bet they keep you busy."

"Yeah, that's an understatement. See these gray hairs?" She pointed to the side of her head. "Each one of them has one of my kids' names on it."

After some more small talk, a police cruiser pulled into the parking lot. "Here's Bill," Susan declared, as both ladies, and Buddy, exited the car.

A middle-aged man in full uniform, including hat, came out of the cruiser. "Hi, Susan," he said in a friendly tone. "It's been a while."

"Yes, it sure has."

Bill bent down to scratch the dog on the head. "Hey Buddy. Looking trim as ever, I see."

Susan snorted with laughter. "Bill, this is my friend Jenny. She's the one who made the discovery."

The officer stood up and outstretched his hand. "Bill Abernathy," he stated, very matter-of-factly. His handshake was firm.

"Jenny Watkins. Nice to meet you."

"So," Bill said, clapping his hands together, "where are these drums?"

"They're in the woods," Jenny said, "Quite a ways back in there."

"Well, before I go poking around back there, let me get official permission. I'll go check with the people who work here and make sure they're okay with it." He headed off into the building.

A surge of nervous energy pulsed through Jenny, which Susan seemed to notice. Susan reached out and rubbed Jenny's back, softly saying, "It'll be okay."

Jenny ran her fingers through her hair, drawing a deep breath. "I'm just a little nervous, that's all. I've got to admit I'm impressed by how calm you are."

"I've been doing this for thirty years," Susan said. "After a while, you get used to it. You'll see."

Bill came out of the building, walking with determination. "Alright, let me get my tools out of the car, and we'll take a look." He opened the trunk and selected a hammer, chisel and crowbar. Once he had what he needed, he turned to the ladies and said, "Okay, where are we headed?"

Susan picked Buddy up and once again tucked him under her arm, gesturing for Jenny to lead the way. Jenny shook all over as she led a now-prepared Bill and Susan back into the woods. This was one of the most nerve-racking moments of Jenny's life.

They arrived at the drums, and Bill dropped his tools to the ground. He selected the hammer and a chisel to break the seal at the top of the first drum. Jenny found that she couldn't watch, turning her back to the scene and placing her hands over her face. She took several steps away, bracing to hear what was inside.

After a minute of tapping and prying, Bill removed the lid of the drum. "Well," he said, "This one looks like it just has some stuff in it."

Relieved, Jenny turned around to inspect the contents of the drum. The top layer had some clothes, which appeared to be t-shirts and jeans, but it was difficult to tell due to the passage of time. Bill pulled out a pair of white bucks shoes, held them up, and said, "These look pretty old. 1950's, maybe?"

115

"Yeah, that would be about right." Jenny felt, at the very least, validated. There was some legitimacy to her finding. She eyed the other drums with a sickened feeling, relieved for the moment to just be looking at belongings.

After removing the shoes and some more clothes, Bill pulled an old camping stove out of the drum. Jenny looked intently at the stove, feeling almost overcome with a wave of familiarity. She pictured a young Elanor and Steve fixing themselves meals over that very stove. She envisioned the laughter, felt the joy. The happiness disappeared quickly, however, when she snapped back into the present, glancing at the other two drums. Her nerves reemerged, and she once again found herself shaking.

After inspecting the rest of the items—some silverware, a pot, a few cans of old food, and some toiletries—Bill declared it was time to look in the next drum. Jenny turned back around to protect herself from the potentially disturbing images, but she listened as she heard Bill pry open the drum. "Okay," she heard Bill say with surprise. "It appears we have ourselves a body."

Jenny sat doubled over on the steps of the maintenance building with her arms wrapped around her mid-section. She looked intently at the ground, not crying, but not able to conjure up any meaningful thought. Bill and Susan were talking near her, but it just sounded like buzzing to her. She remained motionless as Bill approached her.

"The forensics team will be here in a little bit. They'll have some questions for you, but it shouldn't be too intense. This guy apparently died before you were even born, so you're certainly not a suspect. Now who did you say this guy was again?" Bill took out a notepad and a pen.

"Steve O'dell," Jenny whispered.

"And what were the circumstances around his death?"

"He was murdered."

"The ones found in drums usually are," Bill said, but not in a condescending way. "Do you have any idea how he was killed? Or by who?"

"He was shot in the back of the head by a gray haired man on his construction crew. I believe the shooter's name was Arthur

116

Larrabee, but I can't be sure. The man apparently was in cahoots with Luther Whitby, but both men are long since dead by now."

"And nobody reported this guy missing?"

"He was a drifter." Jenny's eyes were still focused on the ground, her voice barely audible. "People assumed he just left town, especially since that's the story the gray-haired man was giving."

"Do you know of any relatives we could use to provide us with some DNA comparison?"

Jenny shook her head slightly. "I know he had some siblings, but he left home at a young age and never looked back. I wouldn't even begin to know where to find them now."

"Did he have any kids?"

"No, sir."

"Okay, thanks," Bill said. His tone then went from professional to sympathetic. "I know this isn't easy. The first one never is. I appreciate your help, Jenny."

Jenny curved her mouth into a feeble smile. "Thanks."

As cars from the forensics team began filing into the parking lot, Bill excused himself to greet his reinforcements. Susan, with a panting Buddy in tow, took a seat next to Jenny. "You doing okay?" she asked.

"I think so," Jenny replied meekly, reaching down to scratch Buddy under the chin. For the moment she was jealous of Buddy's blissful ignorance, wishing her primary concern was a simple token of affection. "I think what's upsetting me most about this is how terribly Steve got treated. It's strange…he died long before I was even born, and I never actually met him, but I've really grown to care about him over the past few weeks. Through what I've seen and the accounts I've heard from Elanor, he seems like he was a great guy." Jenny brushed her hair out of her face. "I hate that he's been out here for sixty years, tossed away like trash. I want more for him than that."

"I know," Susan confessed. "It's easy to become attached to these people. They become such an integral part of your life for a while. You really do start to care about them." She rubbed her hand up and down her leg. "But you can take satisfaction in knowing you are the reason he was found. Thanks to you, he can get a decent burial and be treated with the respect he deserves."

"But nobody will be there. That's the sad thing. Even if he had been found right away, nobody would have gone to his funeral. He had so few people who cared about him. Life dealt this guy such a crappy hand."

Susan spoke solemnly. "You'll get a lot of that, I'm afraid. Sadly, the people who had perfectly happy lives and died peacefully in their sleep aren't the ones who contact you. You're going to be hearing from the people who have been wronged in the most horrible ways. You'll be shocked by what some of these people have gone through. Eventually, though, you learn to distance yourself from it a bit. You can find that middle ground where you still care, but you don't own what you're seeing. It takes a while to get there, though. I know from experience that the first few are tough."

"I felt him get shot," Jenny whispered.

"I've been shot," Susan remarked, smirking at Jenny and playfully leaning into her. "A few times, actually. I've been stabbed. Strangled. Ooh...I was held under water once."

Jenny couldn't help but laugh. "Oh, God, that's awful."

"It was awful. Every bit of it was awful. But you have to remember, it's not your pain. You're just a voice for this person, and I'm quite sure they're grateful to have you."

The commotion from the parking lot grew so loud both women stopped talking, instead looking up at the buzzing crowd. A flurry of people were milling about, each apparently with a unique role. Most of them headed out into the woods, but one gentleman approached Jenny and Susan.

The man posed a series of questions similar to the ones Bill had asked earlier. Jenny felt foolish answering them, realizing she was claiming to know things about people she'd never met and who died before she was even born. She hoped the man interviewing her wasn't a skeptic.

As Bill had predicted, the interview didn't last long. The man took the information back to his car and began filling out a report. Before long a few of the people emerged from the woods carrying white plastic bags, apparently with Steve's belongings in them. They loaded the bags into a truck with the word Forensics written on the side.

Shortly after, three men emerged carrying a drum which, Jenny assumed, contained Steve's remains. She shielded her eyes from the sight and felt Susan's hand on her back. She didn't want to remember Steve this way, but somehow she knew this moment was going to be etched into her memory forever.

She could hear the sound of the drum being loaded into the truck, and she uncovered her eyes to see two more people appearing from the woods with additional white bags. Bill followed closely behind them, approaching Jenny and Susan as he emerged from the trees.

"We found an ID in the third drum," he proclaimed. "The name was Steven O'dell. Good call, Jenny."

Jenny wanted to know what Steve looked like when he was alive and whole. "May I see the picture?"

"I'm afraid that's evidence. Once we're done with the investigation we can release it, but not before."

Jenny nodded with understanding.

"So you say there's no next-of-kin we should notify?" Bill continued.

"He had a girlfriend, who's still alive. I've been in contact with her. She's helped me piece all of this together."

"Might she be able to identify this gray-haired man you spoke of?"

"No, I've already asked her about that. She wasn't sure who he was."

"Well, we'll speak to her briefly," Bill added, "but the reality is that we probably won't spend too much time on it. If the man had gray hair in the 1950s, he's clearly deceased now. Unfortunately we don't have the resources to spend time tracking down killers that we know don't exist anymore. We want to catch the criminals that may reoffend."

"I understand."

Bill took out his pad again. "Can you tell me this woman's name? I'd like to speak with her."

Jenny gave the man Elanor's information, but then added, "Do you mind if I talk to her first? I'd like to be the one to tell her we found Steve's remains."

"That's fine," Bill said. "This isn't a pressing investigation. When you talk to her, please let her know we'll be coming by to ask her a few questions. And since she's the only one who seems to know him, we can find out if she'd like to claim the body and handle the funeral arrangements."

"Okay. Thanks," Jenny said solemnly. "I'm sure she will."

Jenny heard the back door of the forensics truck slam shut and the engine rev. She watched the truck as it began to drive off, paying her respects to the promising young man whose life had been cut way too short. She continued to keep her eyes on the truck until it could no longer be seen, at which time she blinked away tears and looked back at the ground.

She heard the remaining forensic technicians pile into their cars and drive off. Soon she once again sat with just Bill and Susan.

"Well, Jenny," Bill began, "I appreciate everything you've done for us today. Thanks to you we were able to solve a missing person's case we didn't even know we had."

"Glad I could help."

"Let me give you my number," he added. "That way you can call me if you ever have any insight again." Jenny programmed his number into her phone. They exchanged pleasantries, Bill gave Buddy one last scratch on the head, and he drove off.

"Well, I suppose you need a ride home," Susan commented.

"Ucch. Home," Jenny replied. "I don't even want to go home."

"Well, we don't have to. We can go grab a bite to eat or something."

"You know, that would be great. I'm pretty disgusting and sweaty, though."

"I guess a five star restaurant is off the table, then. But we could hit a diner. Nothing beats the blues like greasy food and a milkshake."

"A diner sounds perfect."

Jenny and Susan sat across from each other in a booth in the nearly-deserted diner. Jenny was already on her second glass of water, still feeling grateful for the air conditioning. The scratches and bug bites on her legs were starting to make their presence known, and she longed for a shower. However, the thought of going back to the house and facing Greg was very unappealing.

"I'm glad I have you to talk to," Jenny said. "If all of this was going on and I didn't know anybody who'd been through it, I don't know what I would do."

"I'm glad to help," Susan said. "I know it's not easy."

"It would be a whole lot easier if my husband was supportive. I could really use a hug when I get home, but what I'm going to get instead is an earful about how irresponsible I am for missing our appointment. Not only isn't he making it better, he's making it worse."

"What kind of appointment was it?"

"We were supposed to look at cabinets. You saw the house; we're renovating it, so there are lots of little choices to make. Honestly, I don't really care about cabinets, but to Greg it's a huge deal. The renovation is his number one priority, and in his mind all of this psychic business is getting in the way."

"It really is a shame he doesn't see the value in it," Susan said. "That has to put a strain on your marriage."

With a laugh, Jenny added, "That's an understatement. Unfortunately I've also landed myself in a position where all of my friends are Greg's friends, too, so I can't even really talk to anyone about it. I don't want to put anybody in the middle. Even my own family adores him. I don't want to make any of them uncomfortable, either." Jenny sighed. "I feel like you and Elanor are the only people I know who don't have some kind of allegiance to Greg."

"I've never met the man, so no danger here," Susan declared.

"You might actually be a good friend to have in my corner," Jenny said smiling. "I get the impression that you and your husband have a good relationship."

Susan nodded while shrugging her shoulders. "We do, for the most part. I mean, all couples have their issues, but I think we've got a pretty good thing going."

"It sounds like he respects you, at least. He recognizes the importance of what you do."

Susan made a face. "Well, did I ever tell you how we met?"

"No, you've never said."

"I solved his sister's murder."

Jenny's blood ran cold. "Oh my gosh, I'm so sorry."

"Well, I didn't know her, but it's always tragic when someone so young meets such a horrible fate."

"So what happened?"

"She was a grad student, living alone in an off campus apartment. First floor. Some psychopath pried open her window, came in, and raped and strangled her in her own bed."

"My God, that's horrible."

"I know. But she was a strong-willed one, Adam's sister. She came to me very persistently with the same visions...a shamrock tattoo on the wrist, and a classroom. I worked with Adam to find out what her school schedule was, and we walked around to all of her different classrooms until I found the one she'd showed me. Sure enough, one of her classmates had that tattoo on his wrist. He'd had no criminal history, but some investigation led to a warrant. They got a DNA sample, and it matched the semen left at the crime scene. It was actually one of my simpler cases, to tell you the truth. Christine did a great job of leading the way for me."

"Christine..." Jenny began, "Isn't that your daughter's name?"

"Good memory," Susan said. "Yeah, we named our daughter after her."

"That's awesome."

"I couldn't imagine naming her anything else. But anyway, that's the reason Adam's so supportive of what I do. He knows that when I back out of a dinner reservation, it's because I'm helping someone find a loved one's killer. Having been in that situation, he knows I'm much more needed there than at the restaurant. He's actually very proud of me. He brags about what I do."

Jenny shook her head. "Greg would never brag about what I do. He would brag about himself, but never about me. He would never want to imply that I am better than him in any way."

"It sounds like you've got a good deal of resentment for this guy."

Jenny snorted. "You know what? I do. And it's only come about recently. It wasn't until I realized I had psychic ability that his true colors became apparent to me."

"Let me ask you this. How old were you when you met him?"

"Nineteen."

"That's very young."

"I know. Too young. At the time I thought I was all grown up, but now I realize how immature I was and how backward my priorities were. He was an all-state football player, which made him special in my mind. Now I don't particularly give a shit that he played football in college. It seems trivial, really. Now I just wish he would treat me better."

At that point the waitress arrived with their food. Grabbing a french fry, Jenny grunted with delight as she took a bite. "You're right," she told Susan, "this *does* hit the spot."

"Greasy food always will," Susan replied.

"So," Jenny continued. "What expert advice would you have for a naïve young woman who is just now realizing she married a guy for the wrong reasons?"

"Communication," Susan said flatly. "I know it sounds trite, but it really is the key to any good relationship. You have to be very clear about what you want; men aren't mind readers, that's for sure. You have to be careful of *how* you communicate, though. No name calling. No finger pointing. No tit-for-tat. You don't want to constantly say *you always do this* and *you never do that*. That will only put him on the defensive, and you won't resolve anything. It's best to say things like, *I'd like the marriage to look like this*. That's the best chance you have of initiating a productive conversation."

"Wow," Jenny said. "That's pretty good."

"I've been married for twenty-three years. You have to learn some tricks of the trade along the way."

"Well, I will definitely heed that advice," Jenny declared. "But I'm afraid I've already done something that was a little bit tit-for-tat."

After Susan dropped her off, Jenny walked slowly through the front door, emotionally braced to have a much-needed and very serious conversation with her husband. She found him in the kitchen, holding up little blocks of wood against the existing cabinets, clearly trying to decide which finish looked best.

"Hey," she said softly.

"Hey," he replied.

She took a seat at the kitchen table and said, "Can we talk a minute?"

Greg tossed the blocks of wood onto the counter. "I think we need to." He took a seat at the table.

Jenny let out a sigh and began. "I think we need to come to some agreements about balance."

"I agree."

Jenny was surprised by his answer. "What issues do you think we have with balance?"

"I've already told you," Greg said. "You need to learn to pursue your hobbies in a way that doesn't interfere with our main goal of renovating this house."

After a long, deliberate pause, Jenny calmly posed, "What if I tell you that the renovation is no longer my main goal? How would you feel about that?"

"Well it's pretty obvious that it isn't. And, honestly, I think that sucks. You said this was something you wanted to do back in Kentucky, and now that it's here you're hardly helping at all."

"I've come to realize over the past few weeks that I didn't really want to renovate a house. I knew that was your dream, and I agreed to go along with it because I wanted you to be able to achieve it. Truth be told, a renovation project was never even on my radar until I met you."

"But you still agreed. You should honor that."

"I've agreed to a lot of things. Too many things. I agreed to move here, for you. I agreed to renovate, for you. I agreed to keep my paintings in storage so we could use *your* furniture. I agreed to go to the mountains last summer when I really wanted to go to the beach." Jenny mustered up some strength from somewhere within her. "This marriage needs more balance in the sense that my opinion needs to start counting more."

"But the point is you agreed to all that stuff. You can't turn around and tell me now that you want to change it all."

He had missed the point. "I agreed because I felt like I had to. A large portion of the things we've done in this marriage has been the result of me just agreeing. I'm tired of agreeing. Besides, why can't I change my mind? Marriage is about being flexible."

"Marriage is about sacrifice," Greg countered. "Sometimes you have to do stuff that you don't want if it makes the other person happy."

"I understand that," Jenny said, "but it seems to me that I'm always the one doing the sacrificing."

"Are you kidding?" Greg was growing more heated. "I'm working my balls off fixing up this house so that WE can have enough money to start a family. This project is for US. But every time I turn around you're off doing something that's just for you."

"It's not just for me." Jenny spoke more angrily than she had wanted. "I'm doing this for Elanor. Do you know how grateful she is?"

"Great. An old lady in a nursing home is grateful. That really benefits the marriage."

Jenny took a deep breath and spoke more deliberately. "I have come to realize that, in your mind, something is worth doing only if it benefits you. Can't you ever do something just because it's a kind thing to do? Aren't some things worth doing simply because they'll make someone else happy? Even if it's a stranger?"

"I'm your husband. I should be your number one priority. If you have a choice between doing something that makes me happy or doing something that makes a stranger happy, you should always choose me. You took vows to me, not to a stranger."

"It's not all-or-nothing. It's possible for me be a good wife to you and still be kind to others. That's the balance I'm talking about."

"I'm not saying you can't be kind to others. I'm just saying that it shouldn't come at my expense."

Jenny worked very hard at maintaining her composure as Susan's words rang in the back of her mind. "What I'm proposing is that we come to an agreement where I can spend half my time renovating and half my time working with Elanor."

"Okay, so I'm supposed to spend all my time working on this house, for US, and you spend half your time working for us and half your time doing your own thing. That doesn't seem right."

Jenny felt like she was repeatedly running head first into a brick wall. "But you *want* to do the renovation. I'm suggesting you get to spend one hundred percent of your time doing what you want, and I spend fifty percent of my time doing what I want and fifty percent doing what you want. I think that's more than fair."

"What I want benefits us. What you want benefits you. I hardly call that fair. I think you're being a selfish bitch, truthfully."

Jenny closed her eyes and rubbed her temples. "In productive discussions, you're not supposed to call the other person names."

"Well, in a marriage you're not supposed to make promises you don't keep."

Greg got up angrily from the table, resuming his deliberation over cabinet finishes. Jenny also got up from the table, very slowly, and headed upstairs to take that much-needed shower. She was experiencing so many emotions that she couldn't feel any of them as she mechanically selected clean clothes, undressed, and ran the shower. The water felt very cleansing as it hit her face, washing away the sweat and the dirt and the worries of the day. She stood motionless with her eyes closed, releasing a big exhale, enjoying the feel of the water and counting the days until Greg left for his weekend in Kentucky.

Chapter 14

Sadness choked Jenny as she apprehensively walked through Elanor's open door. Elanor was sleeping with her mouth open, looking closer to death than Jenny cared to see. Jenny tip toed over to her familiar chair, quietly reclining and interlacing her fingers over her stomach. She took a deep breath and enjoyed the silence as Elanor finished her nap.

"Oh, hello, dear," said a scratchy, feeble voice. Elanor cleared her throat. "How long have you been here?"

"I'm not even sure. I dozed off myself," Jenny confessed, stretching her muscles in the chair. "I'm sure it hasn't been long."

"I'm sorry to have kept you waiting. You could have woken me."

"Actually, the nap felt really good. It's been a bit of a rough day."

Elanor pushed the button on the side of her bed which allowed her to sit more upright. She scooted around and adjusted her oxygen tubes as she became more vertical. Once she settled in, she inquired, "Oh? How so?"

Jenny lowered the footrest of her chair so she could lean in closer to Elanor. She placed her hand on top of Elanor's and stated as delicately as she could, "I was led to Steve's remains today."

Elanor didn't respond, but her wide eyes spoke volumes.

"It seems he had been placed in a fifty-five gallon drum which was put behind the facilities maintenance building at Lake Wimsat.

All of his belongings, including his ID, were in two other drums along with it."

Tears began to fill Elanor's eyes. "He's been in a drum?"

Blinking away tears herself, Jenny replied, "I'm afraid so."

"How awful and lonely." Elanor's face looked sadder than Jenny had ever seen, making Jenny desperately wish she could rewrite the past.

"At least he was at Lake Wimsat," Jenny noted, hoping her words were appropriate. "Wasn't that your favorite place?"

"Yes, it sure was," Elanor said incredulously. "I can't believe he's been there all this time. No wonder I felt such serenity when I was there."

"Yes, ma'am. He's always been close to you."

"And that must have been what he meant." Elanor turned to Jenny. "When you heard the words *Lake Wimsat*, he was telling you where he was."

"Indeed he was," Jenny said. "And I completely missed it. He had to get behind the wheel of my car and literally steer me there in order for me to figure it out."

"Is that how you found him?"

"Yes, ma'am. I was driving, and I found myself going the opposite direction of where I needed to go. He led me there, and he did a good job of it, I might add."

"I believe it," Elanor said. "He was good at everything he did."

"Although," Jenny added, "his timing wasn't spectacular."

"What was wrong with his timing?"

"He chose a time when I was on my way to an appointment to look at cabinets with my husband, and when I went the wrong way, it sparked a pretty big fight."

Elanor laughed, which was not the reaction Jenny had been expecting.

"What's so funny?"

"If I know Steve the way I think I do, his timing was one hundred percent deliberate."

"He *meant* to cause a fight between me and Greg?"

"No, not cause a fight. Prove a point. Just like I did when I sent Nancy over to your house. You said before that you don't get to choose when you get contacted; Steve chooses. Well, I'm sure there were plenty of times you were in the car by yourself when he could have led you to his body. But he waited. He waited until your husband was in the car with you." Elanor laughed again. "That is just like Steve."

Surprisingly, Jenny found herself joining in the laughter. She supposed she could add Steve to the list of people who had allegiance to her and not Greg.

"You know," Jenny said reflecting, "I have to admit, I stood up to Greg at that moment in a way I never have in my life."

"Good for you, dear. I'm sure that was Steve's goal."

Unable to wipe the smile from her face, Jenny marveled at the fact that she'd been manipulated, albeit for her own good, by a man who'd been deceased for six decades.

"Well, Miss Elanor, I'm afraid there are a few things that we need to take care of now that Steve's remains have been found. I think you'll agree he deserves a proper burial."

"Actually, no. I don't think he'd like to be buried. I think he'd much prefer to be cremated; it's better for the environment."

"Oh, I'm glad I asked."

Elanor sat up as straight as she could and leaned toward Jenny. "Do you know what I want more than anything, dear? I want you to make sure that Steve and I both get cremated and our ashes get placed in the same urn. Can you do that for me?"

"Absolutely, Miss Elanor."

"And then...I want you to scatter our ashes at Lake Wimsat. Our favorite spot."

"I don't know where that is," Jenny confessed.

"I'm sure Steve will tell you," Elanor said, smiling. Then she shouted, "You hear that, Steve? You've got to show her where our spot is!"

Jenny had to laugh. "And what if he doesn't?"

"Then any old spot will do, as long as it's at the lake. I'll let you use your judgment."

"Okay, Miss Elanor. You got it."

"Well, thank you, dear. I'll call my lawyer and have that drafted in my will. I was going to have my favorite cousin scatter my ashes, but I'll have that changed. She's already taking care of my funeral arrangements; that's enough to ask of someone I wasn't all that close to."

"Do you need my information for the will?"

"Nah. They've got all that at the front desk. They take down every visitor's information when they arrive for their first visit, in case you forgot. That's how I verified everything when I hired Nancy for you. Pretty sneaky, huh?"

"Indeed," Jenny agreed. "You are a resourceful one."

"I ran a magazine. If I wasn't resourceful, I'd have been out of business."

"True. Oh, I nearly forgot. I'm supposed to tell you that some detectives from the police department are going to be coming by to ask you some questions about Steve. They let me be the one to tell you about finding Steve's remains, but they do want to ask you about his family and about his disappearance."

"The disappearance I can help them with. His family? Not so much," Elanor admitted. Then she added, "Are any of the detectives good looking?"

Jenny laughed. "I'm not sure which ones will be coming. You'll have to tell me."

"I'm sure I'll find them good looking, provided they're male and under the age of seventy. My standards are quite low these days."

The women giggled like teenagers. At times it was easy for Jenny to forget that Elanor was two generations older than she, but the paleness of her skin and her frail stature, which seemed to grow weaker with each visit, served as unwelcome reminders. Jenny genuinely wished she had met Elanor earlier in her life and could have spent more time with her. The thought of losing such a cherished friend was becoming increasingly more difficult to bear, although she knew for Elanor the end would have actually been welcome.

After a short while Jenny staged her exit, eager to go home and get some decent sleep after such an exhausting day. The ride home was shortened by swirling thoughts of domestic arguments, ash-spreading, and aptly timed messages from beyond. At home she found herself with very little energy left for confrontation, so she avoided Greg and headed upstairs to bed.

"Hello?" Jenny hoped her voice sounded nonchalant as she answered the phone, masking her excitement about talking to Zack. With Greg working mere feet away from her, she didn't want to appear too eager.

130

"Hi, Jenny? It's Zack Larrabee."

"Hi, how are you?"

"I'm doing great. I've got a little information here you might like to know."

Jenny's pulse quickened. "That's fantastic."

"I got a photograph of Arthur, so it might be better if we met in person somewhere."

Jenny liked that idea, although she was sure Greg would have been a lot less thrilled about it if he knew. She glanced in her husband's direction, feeling horribly transparent, and declared, "Sure. Where would you like to meet?"

Greg looked up from his work for a second, meeting Jenny's gaze, and then shook his head disapprovingly as he went back to work. He didn't even know she was arranging to meet an eligible bachelor; she couldn't imagine how upset he would have been if he had known the full truth.

"I'm actually kind of hungry. There's a sub shop a few doors down from Larrabee Homes. Do you want to meet there and grab a bite?"

Ordinarily Jenny would have declined out of respect for her marriage, but she had very little of that left. "Perfect. I'll be there in about fifteen minutes?"

"Great. See you there."

As much as she would have liked to just walk out the door, Jenny felt as if she owed Greg an explanation. "I'm meeting with the folks at Larrabee and Sons Custom Homes. They're going to give me some information about who worked on the construction crew with Steve right before he died."

"Okay, bye," Greg said coldly.

Perhaps Greg didn't realize his immature behavior only made Zack seem more appealing in Jenny's mind. Zack appreciated her psychic ability. He bragged about his sister's knack for baking. He was personable. Greg, on the other hand, had been nothing but a big, fat pain in the ass lately. The scales were definitely tipping in Zack's favor.

Jenny grabbed her keys and headed out the door, eager to have a pleasant lunch and see a first-hand picture of Arthur Larrabee. She recalled the image of the gray-haired man from her vision, making sure she'd be able to recognize him once she saw the picture. The visual was easy to conjure up; that was a face she wouldn't soon forget.

She found the sub shop rather easily, but Zack wasn't there when she arrived. She checked the time; she had been perfectly punctual. She waited at the shop for what seemed like an eternity, unsure of whether to be angry or worried, until Zack pulled into the parking lot almost fifteen minutes late.

"Hey," he said immediately. "Sorry. I got held up." He was dressed in a tie-dye shirt and khaki shorts, fueling Jenny's suspicion that he didn't belong in a dress shirt and tie.

"That's okay," Jenny said. "It happens to the best of us." While she said it was okay, she had to admit Zack was substantially less attractive than he'd been just twenty minutes earlier.

Zack pulled a manila envelope out of his passenger seat and approached the shop's entrance with it tucked under his arm. Jenny eyed the package with excitement; this was the information she'd been waiting for. She couldn't wait to go back and provide confirmation to Elanor, granting her the peace she so desperately longed for before she passed.

Jenny remained patient as the two ordered their sandwiches, eventually taking a seat in a booth by a window. "I bet you're excited to see this," Zack said, opening up the envelope.

Jenny nodded with wide eyes. "Excited isn't the word."

"Well, I'll start with the picture of Arthur." He handed Jenny a paper copy of an old black-and-white photo. When she flipped the page around to face her, her jaw hit the ground.

"Oh my God," Jenny said. "This isn't him."

Chapter 15

"What do you mean it isn't him?" Zack asked.

"It isn't him. It's not the guy from my vision." She rubbed her hand down her face, squeezing her chin at the bottom. "Are you *sure* this is a picture of Arthur?"

"Positive. It had his name and the date written on the back of the original. My dad even verified it was him."

Jenny placed her head in her hands, suddenly developing a headache. "I had given her answers." Again, Jenny was really talking to herself, but doing so out loud.

"Uh-oh. You told Elanor that Arthur had done it?"

"Yup," Jenny let out a loud exhale. "I guess I should have waited until I had proof. I was just so excited."

"Well, I also have the name of the foreman of the crew, if that'll help. I couldn't get a list of all the workers, but we do keep records of whose team it was."

Jenny's spirits picked back up. "Who was it?"

Zack looked at the notes on his paper. "It says here that the foreman of the crew was Brian Larrabee."

Jenny looked at Zack in disbelief. "Who is Brian?"

Zack smiled proudly. "I didn't know, so I took the liberty of doing a little research. He was Arthur's brother."

"Do you have a picture of him?"

Zack's pride disappeared. "No."

"And you have no idea who could have been working on his crew?"

"No."

Jenny thought silently for a moment. "Could you possibly get a picture of Brian?"

"I could try."

That would have to be good enough for now, Jenny surmised. Disappointed, she thought about taking a bite of her sandwich, but her appetite had vanished. She held her tray out to Zack. "You want this? I can't eat."

"I'll never turn down food. You sure you don't want it?"

"Positive. Although, if that picture had been of the guy from my vision, I'd have probably gone back for seconds."

Zack took the sandwich off of her tray and placed it on his own. "So are you going to tell Elanor that you were wrong? Or are you just going to let her believe what she believes?"

Jenny deliberated to no avail. "I don't know. What do you think I should do?"

"I'd leave it be," Zack said, wasting no time on Jenny's sandwich. "No sense upsetting her if she's at peace."

"I do agree with that, on one hand," Jenny said, "But on the other hand you've got to know Elanor. She's a straight-shooter. She'd be furious with me if she knew I was hiding the truth."

Zack grunted as he swallowed. "That is a tough one. I'm glad I'm not in your shoes." He flashed that smile of his, instantly knocking Jenny's stress level down a few notches.

Enjoying the brief moment of levity, Jenny decided to perpetuate it. "So, do you like working for your family's business?"

"In a word? No."

"Really?" Jenny replied. "That answer surprises me."

"Did I act like I liked my job when you met with me?"

Jenny thought back to their first encounter. "You didn't act like you hated it."

"Then I'm a good actor."

Jenny smiled. "Then why do you do it?"

"Because I'm a Larrabee. And I have a penis." He took a drink through his straw. "In my family, as soon as a boy sprouts his first pimple, they put a hammer in his hand. He swings that around until he turns 25, and then they take it back out of his hand and give him some sort of managerial job. That's how it goes. I just happened to get a desk job, probably because I sucked at carpentry. Or perhaps because I'm so good looking I attract customers." He posed like a model.

"Oh, it has to be the latter," Jenny said jokingly.

"Definitely," Zack agreed.

"If you hate it, why don't you do something different?"

"Because I'm a Larrabee." He smiled. "And I have a penis. Haven't we been through this?"

"Umm," Jenny began, "last I checked this was America. You have the right to pick your own career."

"Not in my family."

"What are they going to do to you? Disown you?"

Zack looked intently at Jenny. "That's exactly what they would do."

"That sucks."

"To be fair," he continued, "I'd probably hate any job I had. I hate work in general." Zack was no longer attractive to Jenny. "The good part about my job is that it isn't nine to five. My hours vary, which gives me a little bit of freedom that most people don't have."

"I get that. I'm a teacher, so I have summers off."

"I thought you were a psychic."

"Being psychic doesn't pay the bills."

"Touché." He tipped his soda cup in her direction. "But it's still very cool."

Jenny enjoyed the small talk as Zack finished both of his sandwiches. She was actually relieved her attraction toward him had subsided; that could have only led to trouble. He did, however, seem like a fun guy to have as a friend, and she was glad that she met him.

As they gathered up their trash and headed for the door, Zack agreed to investigate Brian a little more and report his findings back to Jenny. She hoped that would bring some answers, but she was becoming discouraged. This mystery certainly wasn't as cut and dry as it had seemed.

As she drove home, she considered how ridiculous it was that Zack worked a job he didn't like simply because his family expected him to. The solution seemed obvious to Jenny--tell the family he doesn't want to be in the construction business and find a different job. If the family didn't like it, too bad. They'd have to get over it.

However, there was Jenny, the queen of the hypocrites, heading home to a renovation project she didn't enjoy and a husband who didn't respect her opinion. To an outsider, her solution would probably have been equally as simple. Get out. Move on. Find a new place and be happy. But she had taken a vow. She had financial commitments. Neither she nor Greg could afford that house by themselves, and nobody would buy it looking the way it did. She suddenly gained more sympathy for Zack's situation. She was sure it, too, was more complicated than it appeared on the surface.

Jenny marveled at how much she resembled Steve's description of 'most people.' She was mechanically going through life, unhappily doing what she was supposed to, feeling like she had very few choices at this point. Despite Steve's nomadic lifestyle, perhaps he *had* been one of the luckiest people in the world. At least he had controlled his own destiny, albeit for a short time.

Jenny also developed an even greater respect for Elanor, who was brave enough to take the leap that she and Zack seemingly couldn't. Although, Jenny did have to stop and give herself credit for how far she'd come already. Maybe she wasn't exactly where she wanted to be yet, but she was definitely a different person than she'd been back in Kentucky.

"Kentucky," she said out loud, forgetting her pledge to stop talking to herself. The following morning Greg was scheduled to leave for his bachelor party weekend. Jenny felt the weight of the world lift off of her shoulders.

After her lunch with Zack, Jenny spent eight straight hours working on the house, stopping only to grab a quick bite for dinner. She had to admit they were making good progress. Soon enough they would be on the cosmetic work and Jenny would like the renovation process a whole lot better.

Having worked ridiculously hard for most of the day, Jenny was exhausted come evening. She showered off the sweat and dirt of the day, put on her pajamas, and climbed mercifully into bed.

Soon she found herself flying. Water was below her, whizzing by at breakneck speed. She approached the water's edge and hovered there, seeing a young couple on a blanket. The image was blurry, as if she was seeing it through water. The woman was blond; the young man had dark hair. She could hear their voices but couldn't make out the words. The man got on one knee, holding out an offering to the woman. Jenny flew closer, circling—hoping. "Please don't," Jenny felt herself say. "Please don't do this."

After a moment the man gathered his belongings and stormed off. Jenny felt flooded with relief.

The woman sat alone. Jenny hovered near, feeling peace-- unity. *"Don't worry,"* ran through Jenny as she tried to provide the woman with invisible comfort. *"You're not alone. I'm here. I'm waiting for you. As long as you don't leave me, we'll have eternity. Just don't leave me."*

Jenny felt a demented blend of guilt and happiness. Love, she knew, didn't mean wishing loneliness on the other person. But Jenny was enlightened. She knew how it could be. They could be together forever, if only the woman could remain unattached during this lifetime.

Jenny would just have to make sure the woman didn't fall in love again.

Jenny sat up with a gasp. She looked around, happy to discover that she was no longer a floating entity, but rather alive and whole in her own bed. She lowered her shoulders as she relaxed, realizing what had just happened. In her visions she'd always had Steve's perspective, and this was no different.

Now she just knew what the viewpoint looked like from the other side.

Chapter 16

By the time Jenny woke up in the morning, Greg was putting the finishing touches on his packing.

She rolled over groggily. "Hey. What time are you heading out of here?"

"Soon," he said. "I just have a few more things to collect and I'll be on my way." He closed a drawer. "So what are you planning to do today?"

"Well, I'm going to start with a trip to Maple Estates." Jenny saw no point in lying anymore.

"I should have known."

He disgusted her. Feeling the desire to be away from him, she got out of bed and headed toward the bathroom. "Do you have what you need from in here? I want to shower, but I can wait if you're not done."

"No, I'm good. Go ahead and shower."

Jenny walked into the bathroom. No kiss goodbye. No hug. No *I love you*. Things had certainly changed in the past few weeks.

Jenny showered slowly despite her eagerness to get to Maple Estates. She wanted to be sure Greg was gone by the time she was done, so she took far more time than necessary. Her plan had worked; when she emerged from the shower, Greg's car was already gone from the driveway.

Her mood immediately escalated. The black cloud that hung over the house had lifted, and the broken-down shit-hole they lived in actually didn't seem quite so bad. Maybe the animosity she'd felt toward the house had less to do with the crumbling walls and more to do with the man who inhabited them.

Feeling more free than she had in ages, Jenny hummed as she fixed herself breakfast. Three whole days, she thought. Three whole days without feeling the need to explain her every move. This was the best she had felt in ages.

When Jenny finished up her breakfast, she delighted in leaving the dirty dishes in the sink. "I'm going to do that *later,*" she said as she exaggeratedly turned up her nose and walked away. With a quick brush of her teeth, she grabbed her purse and headed out the door. She sang off key to the radio for the entire length of the ride, making up words to the songs she didn't know. The levity made the ride seem shorter than usual, and before she knew it the sign for Maple Estates appeared before her. Once through the double doors, she practically skipped down to Elanor's room but was taken aback when she walked through the doorway.

Elanor looked markedly more ill than she ever had before. She was lying flat on the bed, tubes still in her nose, color drained from her face. Jenny froze for a moment, wondering if Elanor had actually passed away without anyone knowing it yet. Slowly she took several steps closer, eventually finding that Elanor was, in fact, breathing and was merely asleep.

Jenny covered her heart with her hands, bowing her head and taking a few silent gasps of relief. Once she gathered her composure, she sat in the recliner, patiently waiting for Elanor to wake up. Within a few minutes Elanor opened her eyes, at first unaware that Jenny was even there.

"Good morning, sleepy head," Jenny said.

"Oh!" Elanor exclaimed with a start. After a weak laugh she added, "I didn't see you there."

"Surprise!" Jenny waved her hands in the air.

"Surprise indeed." Elanor's eyes twinkled. "I just nearly shit my pants." Even though her health was declining, her spunk remained unaffected. Jenny was surely going to miss her friend.

"Sorry," Jenny remarked. "Maybe I should wear a bell around my neck so you can hear me coming."

Elanor laughed. "Well, now that you've sufficiently scared the crap out of me, to what do I owe the pleasure this morning?" Jenny noted that for the first time, Elanor did not make the attempt to sit upright; she continued the conversation lying down.

"I just wanted to see if I have something straight."

"Okay, shoot."

"A young blond woman and a dark haired young man were sitting on a blanket by the side of a lake. The man offered the woman a ring, which she declined, causing the man to storm off. The woman sat alone on the side of the water for quite some time…"

"Oh my God," Elanor whispered. "Did I tell you that?"

"No, ma'am," Jenny said softly, affectionately smoothing out an unruly patch of Elanor's hair. "I watched it." Jenny smiled kindly at Elanor. "It appears Steve was there with you that day."

Elanor closed her eyes as a tear dripped slowly down to her pillow.

"But that's not the best part," Jenny added delicately. "I got to know what he was thinking. It appears he is waiting for you, Miss Elanor."

Elanor opened her eyes again. "He's waiting for me?"

"Yes. He is," Jenny whispered. "He unwilling to cross over until you can do it with him. That's why he's able to communicate with me—he isn't fully gone yet."

Elanor silently contemplated Jenny's words, looking far more serious than Jenny cared to see.

Jenny made her tone less sober to lighten the mood. "In fact, one of his goals was to make sure you never fell in love with anyone else. He wanted you to wait for him, just like he was waiting for you, so he lingered—hovered—just enough to make sure you never gave your heart to another man." Elanor didn't respond, so Jenny continued. "According to my calculations, you weren't made of stone, like you claim. You just lived your life with a partner you couldn't see."

"So he's been around? All this time?"

"Yes, ma'am."

Elanor resumed her silence, eventually adding, "Is he here now?"

"I'm afraid I don't know that. I only see the little snippets he allows me to see. I don't ever feel his presence." Jenny smiled. "But it *is* possible."

"And I get to be with him after I die?" Elanor's eyes grew teary again.

"For eternity." Jenny stroked Elanor's hand.

From the confines of her bed, Elanor looked so painfully fragile. "Do you know how happy this makes me?" She wiped her tears away with her hand.

Jenny got up and retrieved a tissue box from the kitchen counter. Pulling a few out and handing them to Elanor, she replied, "I'm glad."

"I'm serious," Elanor said, dabbing at her eyes. "This changes everything." She looked squarely at Jenny. "Do you know what it's been like in here? Do you know how it feels to know that every good thing that's ever going to happen in your life has already happened? Before you came into my life, the only things I had to look forward to were visits from the handyman and Cherry Jello night. But now...now I know that when I die I get to be with Steve again. Now death isn't just an end to my misery, it's actually a beginning—the beginning of something wonderful." Tears flowed readily. "I can't thank you enough for that."

"Don't thank me," Jenny reminded her. "I'm just the vehicle, remember? Steve's the driver. I don't write the messages, I just deliver them."

"Modest, as always." Elanor gestured for another tissue, which Jenny provided. "You're a remarkable young woman." Elanor cleaned herself off and regained some control of her emotions. "Good gracious. I'm getting all worked up this morning." She threw her used tissues into a pail that Jenny had held up for her, and then she added in her usual humorous tone, "Does this mean Steve sabotaged all of my relationships?"

Jenny giggled. "I believe it does."

"Fucker," Elanor remarked, then shouted louder. "Fucker! You hear that Steve? You're a fucker. All these years I thought I was cold-hearted, and it was you all along, you selfish bastard."

Jenny laughed with every word Elanor spoke. A spitfire until the very end.

With a sigh and subsequent release of emotion, Elanor asked, "Were you able to see that picture of Arthur?"

Jenny froze. With her latest vision, she had forgotten all about the photograph. She still hadn't decided how she was going to handle

141

that, but one look into Elanor's red, puffy eyes made her choice clear. "No, I haven't gotten that yet."

"Let me know when you do," Elanor said. "And then bring it in here so I can throw darts at it."

Jenny smiled. "Will do."

Jenny arrived back at the house at 11:30, making sure she was home in time for the noon to 2:00 window the Red Cross folks had given her. She fixed herself a sandwich and lounged on the couch while eating, enjoying the last bit of comfort the living room would provide for the next few weeks. She flipped through the channels on the television until the doorbell rang, at which time she greeted the two men dressed in Red Cross uniforms.

"Good day, ma'am," one of them said, "We're here for the furniture."

"Yes, nice to see you." Jenny replied. "Thanks for coming out on such a hot day."

"There's no other kind of day in Georgia in the summer."

Jenny showed the men which pieces they would be taking, which was pretty much everything. "You're not going to have any furniture left when we're done," the other man noted.

"We have new furniture coming," Jenny said. "In the meantime we've got folding tables and chairs." Then she added, "How's the family doing?"

"The family from the fire?"

Jenny nodded. "Yes sir."

"They're okay. They're glad no one was hurt, but they lost everything. No renter's insurance." The man shook his head. "Gotta have renter's insurance."

"Well, now they have some furniture."

"Yes ma'am, thanks to you. They also have a lot of clothes and toys for the kids that people donated. It's nice to see how kind people can be in the face of tragedy."

"Yes," Jenny noted, "it sure is."

The workers proceeded to take out all of the furniture except the television and the bedroom set, although Jenny gave them the bedding. At the end of it all, the larger of the two men asked Jenny to sign a form, and then he looked at her with a smile. "Thank you for doing this. The family will be so happy. God bless you."

"You as well," Jenny replied. As she closed the door behind them, she couldn't help but smile. Her house looked as empty as the day she moved in, but her spirit felt full. Very little in life could rival the joy of giving to those who truly needed it.

She'd have to remember this feeling when Greg got home and realized she gave the furniture away. She grimaced when she remembered Susan advising against tit-for-tat, but these wheels had already been put into motion before that greasy meal at the diner. "Oh well," she muttered, "What's done is done." She felt too good to let Greg's inevitable disapproval get her down. She headed out to the garage for a folding chair, setting it down in the middle of the empty living room.

As she sat awkwardly in the chair, she thought about Zack, hoping he too would one day get the courage to stand his ground. It didn't seem right anyone born a Larrabee had to go into construction, like it or not.

"Wait a minute," she said standing up. "Wait a minute. Wait a minute. Wait a minute." After a moment of deliberation she rushed to the phone and dialed. Two rings later she heard, "Hey Jenny."

"Hey, Zack. How's it going?"

"Eh," he replied. "I'm at work."

"Sorry to hear that," Jenny said. "Listen, I just had a thought. You said all Larrabees have to work for the company, right?"

"Just the ones with penises." Jenny heard an angry voice in the background. "Oh, sorry dad. It's just a friend."

Jenny couldn't help but smirk.

"God, I hate this fucking place," Zack whispered into the phone.

"I'm sorry, but that was funny. Anyway, did Brian happen to have any sons? And if so, would it be a safe assumption that they would have worked on his crew?"

"One step ahead of you," Zack said, his pride in his ability to play detective fully restored. "He had three sons: Everett, Richard and John. I'm in the middle of doing some digging, but I was able to find out that Everett died a while ago. Richard is alive and well but lives about three hours away. I was just looking into John's whereabouts when you called. I'm hoping he's local so we can talk to him easily. If not, it looks like we'll have to take a road trip so we can have a talk with Richard."

143

Jenny was flattered. "You'd actually go with me?"

"Are you kidding?" Zack asked. "This is the coolest thing ever. I'd be bummed if you went without me."

Considering Zack's appeal as a romantic prospect had taken a nose dive in the sub shop, Jenny didn't feel the least bit funny about spending a day with him. "I really appreciate that," she said, "but it would still be nice if John ends up living closer and we don't have to spend six hours in the car."

"Yeah, it would be," Zack began. "But if we do need to take a road trip, are you available tomorrow? It's my only day off for a while."

"Tomorrow would be ideal, actually. Just let me know if we need to go."

"Give me a little bit of time, and I'll give you a call when I find out. Sound good?"

"Sounds perfect. Thanks, Zack."

"You bet."

Jenny hung up the phone with renewed optimism, although she was uncertain how long Zack would take to find John's whereabouts. To kill some time, she hopped in her car and headed out to a gas station with a convenience store, picking up her first issue of *Choices* magazine. She returned home, sat uncomfortably in her folding chair, and opened the pages.

Her focus first turned to an article entitled, 'Know Your Worth.' The segment was directed toward working women, advising them not to settle for too little in the workplace, but she was able to translate those same principles into her own life. That had been her problem. She didn't know her worth until recently, and she was willing to settle for much less than she had deserved in her marriage. The article offered advice on how to negotiate with an employer in order to get a higher salary. Jenny didn't want a higher salary; she wanted her husband to regard her as an equal.

As she contemplated the article, her phone rang. "Well hello, Zack. Did you find anything out about John?"

"Yup," he replied. "Dead as a doornail. You ready for a road trip?"

Chapter 17

Zack was supposed to be at Jenny's house at 9:00. At 9:40, he finally arrived. Jenny got into his car, and this time he offered no apology for being late. He also had a coffee and doughnuts for himself, and none for Jenny. She smirked at his immaturity. The fact that this adorable man was a bachelor made sense to her now; he definitely wasn't marriage material.

"You ready?" he asked.

"Absolutely. Does Richard know we're coming?"

"Yup. I checked with him yesterday. I didn't want to drive all the way out there and have him not be home." Zack pulled out of the driveway and started on his way.

"Good call. Does he know what this is about?"

"I told him it was about one of his fellow crew members getting murdered, and he said he remembered it."

"How could he remember it when no one knew he was murdered until now?"

"I guess we're about to find out."

Jenny felt a twinge of excitement which she kept subdued, realizing this promising lead might also turn out to be another dead end.

"Have you ever met Richard before?" Jenny asked.

"Maybe, but if I did I don't remember. We're a huge family, and we often have a lot of gatherings where I don't know everybody. He's probably been at a few of those, but I generally stick with people that are my own age at those things."

"You know, I usually do that too, but now that I've met Elanor I may change my tune."

"Oh yeah?"

"Let me tell you, that woman's a trip." Jenny told Zack all about Elanor, including some of the crass things she'd said during the visits.

"She sounds like quite a woman," Zack admitted.

"She sure is," Jenny replied sadly. "I'm going to miss her when she's gone."

Zack glanced at Jenny as he drove, offering her a sympathetic smile. Irresponsible as he may have been, he was indeed a nice guy.

"So," Jenny began in a friendlier tone. "Are there any Mrs. Zack Larrabees running around? Or Zack Larrabee Juniors?"

Zack laughed. "No. No wife, and I don't think I have kids. Guys can never be sure, though."

"Okay, that's scary," Jenny replied. "You got a girlfriend?"

"No, but I'm working on one."

Jenny felt a hint of worry, hoping she wasn't the girl he was working on. "Oh yeah? Who's the lucky lady?"

"She's a waitress at a restaurant I like to go to."

Relief.

"She's young, though," Zack continued. "She's only like, twenty one or twenty two."

"How old are you?"

"Twenty nine."

"That's not so bad. Age is just a number. Maturity level is what counts."

Zack laughed. "Then we're good. I operate at about eighteen or nineteen."

"At least you can admit that," Jenny noted. "Have you asked her out yet?"

"No. That's what I'm working on."

"What's the hold up?"

"I want to be sure she'll say yes if I ask."

The logic seemed odd to Jenny. "You know, it's flattering to a girl when someone asks her out, even if she's not interested. Well, unless the guy is creepy, which you're not. I think you should ask her. What's the worst that can happen?"

"She'll laugh in my face. And then she'll get all of the restaurant patrons to come over and laugh in my face, too."

Jenny was amused by the visual. "Do you really think that's what will happen?"

"No, but it could."

"I think you have a better chance of being struck by lightning." Jenny slid her feet out of her flip flops and crossed her legs on the passenger seat. "What if I made it a bet? Would it be easier to ask her out if it was a dare?"

"Actually, it would."

"Okay, then, here goes," Jenny said. "If you ask her out within a week, I'll give you the gas money for this trip. If you weenie out, you're paying for it."

"A week?"

"Yes. A week. Any more than that and you run the risk of some other dude coming in and snatching her up. So do we have a deal?"

Zack sighed. "Deal." He reached his right hand out and Jenny shook it.

"Now can I offer you some advice if she says yes?"

"Please do. I seem to fuck up every date I go on."

Jenny wasn't surprised. She told him about the importance of punctuality, responsibility, and consideration. She pointed out that a phone call this morning would have been appropriate, letting her know he was running late and also offering to pick her up a coffee or doughnut as well. "Those are the kinds of things that go a long way," Jenny concluded.

"You know, that never would have occurred to me." Again he flashed Jenny a sideways smile. "You're a good friend to have in my corner."

"Just name your first born daughter after me and we'll call it even."

The conversation flowed lightly the rest of the way to Richard's house. The three hour trip went by rather quickly, and before she knew it they had arrived.

Jenny could feel her stomach flutter as she and Zack got out of the car. "I'm nervous."

"Nothing to worry about," Zack replied as they headed up the sidewalk.

"What if he's mean?"

"He's, like, eighty."

"Yeah, I know. Sometimes old people can be nasty."

They arrived at the front step and Zack pressed the doorbell. "If he starts throwing punches, I think we can take him."

"But what if he has a gun? Then what will…"

The door opened to reveal an elderly man dressed in long pants and a sweater. "Uncle Richard?" Zack asked.

Jenny gave Zack a strange look; Richard wasn't his uncle.

"Yes," Richard said nonetheless. "You must be Zack. Come on in." He backed up slowly to let Zack and Jenny in. The house was sweltering.

"This is Jenny," Zack said. "She's a psychic."

Jenny felt awkward as she held out her hand. "Hi, nice to meet you."

Richard shook her hand and eyed her suspiciously. "A psychic, huh? You can read minds?"

Jenny shook her head, wishing Zack hadn't said anything. "No, not exactly. I just get a feel for things."

"Well, go on, have a seat," Richard said, gesturing toward the couch. He sat down in a worn old chair that was clearly his favorite.

Jenny looked around as she and Zack sat on the sofa. "You have a lovely home."

"Built it myself," Richard said, "back in 1962. It's held up real good."

"It certainly has," Jenny replied politely. Her eyes scanned the room until they fell on an old framed photograph on the end table. The black and white picture featured a young couple on their wedding day; the style of dress the bride wore indicated the picture was from the 1920s. While she couldn't tell for sure because she was too far away, Jenny believed the groom could be a younger version of the gray-haired man from her vision.

Zack was busy eyeing the handiwork. "Egg and dart, huh? Nice touch."

"It was expensive but worth it," Richard said.

Based on where the two Larrabees held their gazes, Jenny surmised they were talking about the crown molding.

"I see you have judge's paneling in the dining room, too," Zack noted.

Richard went on a rather lengthy tangent about how he decided upon that particular style of paneling. Jenny couldn't help but smile; Zack knew exactly which buttons to push to get Richard comfortable and talking. Perhaps this was some construction code of honor she wasn't familiar with; she was grateful to have Zack there.

After the comments about the house were over, Jenny posed a question. "Mr. Larrabee, do you mind if I ask about that picture on your end table?"

Richard glanced in the direction of the photo. "That one? What about it?"

"Who are they?"

"Those are my parents, on their wedding day."

Jenny flashed what she hoped was a subtle glance in Zack's direction. She scooted down to the end of the couch, taking a closer look at the smiling couple. Indeed, she was looking squarely in the face of the man who eventually went on to kill Steve O'dell.

"That's a lovely picture," she commented, resuming her original place back on the couch. Another subtle glance and nod in Zack's direction let him know she'd found their man.

Richard looked solemn. "I know what you guys are here for."

Feeling uncomfortable, Jenny delicately stated, "Any information you can give us would be greatly appreciated."

"Y'all aren't cops, are you?"

"I'm a Larrabee," Zack said. "I build houses."

Jenny raised her hand. "I teach fourth grade."

Richard sighed and made a grunting sound. "You know, when you get to be my age, you start thinking about your life and what you done. You like to think that what you done is good, and when you meet your maker you'll get the green light to go on to heaven." He looked sadly at Jenny and Zack. "My wife's there, you know. She died a few years ago, and she was an amazing woman. There's no doubt she's in heaven. She never done nothing bad to nobody."

Zack and Jenny sat quietly, waiting for Richard to continue.

"But I got this thing…this one thing I done that might mean I don't get to be with Beth after all." Tears formed in Richard's eyes. "I can't stand the thought of never seeing her again."

Jenny felt her heart splitting in two.

"We're not here to judge you, Uncle Richard. We are just trying to find out what happened."

"It ain't *your* judgment I'm worried about."

Jenny leaned forward in her chair and spoke softly. "Mr. Larrabee, what's done is done. You can't change the past. But there's a woman in a nursing home who doesn't have much time left…she's looking to find out what happened to her boyfriend back in 1954. All she wants is answers, and then she'll feel like she can die peacefully. I know you can't take back the events from sixty years ago, but you can do the right thing now and give a woman some solace in her final days." Jenny tried to make eye contact with Richard, but he was looking at his lap. "Besides," she added, "I know you didn't do it."

With that Richard did look up at Jenny, who added, "But I know who did." She gestured her head in the direction of the photograph. Tears fell freely from Richard's eyes at that point; he grabbed some tissues from the coffee table and covered his face with them.

"I'm glad this secret isn't going to die with me," Richard said feebly. "It's been eating me up since I was a kid. I never told nobody what happened, not even Beth. My brothers never said nothing neither. They took this secret to their graves."

"What happened, Mr. Larrabee?"

With a sigh Richard gained some composure and began his story. "My dad…he used to gamble a lot. When I was a kid it wasn't that bad, I don't think. But as I got older, it got worse. By the time I was a teenager, it got so bad we didn't have any money. My uncle Arthur offered my father a job with his construction company. My dad made me and my brothers quit school and work for him, too. My uncle used to pay us for working for him, but my dad would take the money. He called it rent. There were always houses to build, so business was good. Uncle Arthur was certainly living high on the hog, but we never knew where our next meal was coming from. And this went on for years.

"My parents used to fight a lot. They didn't think we could hear them, but we could. My mom was threatening to leave and take us boys with her, saying she couldn't take no more. My dad just kept saying he could get us out of it. He kept on talking about these 'sure things' he could bet on. How he couldn't lose. How if he could just borrow a little bit of money, he'd be able to make ten times that much." Richard wiped some tears from his cheeks. "He thought he could gamble his way out of the hole."

150

At that point Richard let out a sigh that had clearly been in him for decades. "Back in 1954 I was seventeen years old. I remember my dad came up to my brothers and me one Saturday morning and told us we needed to go somewhere. He told us not to say nothing, just get in the truck. We knew something was up, but we did what he said. In the truck he just kept telling us that we needed to keep our mouths shut about what we were about to do. If we said anything to anyone, everyone in the family would go to jail. Yeah, I was pretty scared.

"He drove us to the site on Meadowbrook Road. It was where we had been working. Everything seemed normal except there was a fifty five gallon drum sitting there. He told us it was too heavy for him to lift by himself, and he needed our help putting it in the truck. We didn't know what was in it. We didn't want to know what was in it. We knew it was something bad.

"Later that night, when it got dark out, my dad told us we needed to go back out again. We went to this house that had a door in the back. My dad popped off the door knob and we went in. He told us to take everything we could find out of there. I thought we were stealing, but I did as I was told. My brothers did too. We were too scared not to.

"We ended up putting all that stuff into to some other drums and sealing them up. My dad put the doorknob back on like we'd never been there. Then, in the middle of the night we drove the drums out to some building somewhere. We walked them pretty far out into the woods and left them there." Richard shook his head. "I didn't know what I done, but I knew it was bad.

"On the way home my dad said again that if we breathed a word of this to anyone, we'd all be done for. I knew I wasn't going to say nothing. My brothers didn't say nothing neither.

"But after that, things got much better at home. We had money. My mom and dad stopped fighting. My dad stopped taking the money we earned from Uncle Arthur. I knew it had to be because of what we done that night, so I guess in a way I was glad I did it, whatever it was. It sure made my life better.

"I did notice that one guy from work stopped showing up after that. A few guys asked where he'd gone, and my dad just said he'd left town. I guess if I thought about it I'd know something wasn't right, but I didn't let myself think about it." He looked squarely at

Jenny and Zack. "I'm pretty sure I know what was in that drum now that you said there was a murder."

"Yes," Jenny said softly. "Unfortunately his remains were found in a drum not too long ago."

Richard sobbed freely for a few minutes, ripping Jenny's soul in half. "Mr. Larrabee," she added. "Might I say something?"

Richard didn't agree, but he didn't protest, so Jenny continued.

"I really don't think you should let this eat you up. Truly. This wasn't your idea…you were just a kid doing as you were told." Jenny hoped she wasn't overstepping her bounds. "I actually think it was unfair for your father to put you in that position."

Jenny's words seemed to provide Richard with some comfort. The tears slowed to a stop, and he looked up at his two guests on the couch. "That's what I've tried to tell myself over the years, but I wasn't sure if I believed it."

"Believe it," Jenny said sincerely. "It's the absolute truth."

Richard uncomfortably shifted his position in his chair. "Now that I've given you two your answers, can you clear up something for me?"

"Absolutely," Jenny said. "That is, if we can."

"Who was that guy in the drum, and who was willing to pay that much to make him disappear?"

Jenny felt that after all those years of guilt Richard had endured, he deserved to hear the truth. She recited the entire story, pulling out no stops, noting Richard grimaced every time she talked about the love between Elanor and Steve. At the end of the account, Richard silently nodded with understanding.

"You know," he began, "It actually feels pretty good to get this off my chest."

"I imagine it does. That's quite a secret you've had to harbor," Jenny replied. "Honestly, the way I see it, you were just as much of a victim in this crime as Steve was."

"You know," Richard began, "there was one other victim in this crime."

Jenny's blood ran cold. "Who?"

"My father." Richard looked Jenny in the eye. "He committed suicide four months after this happened."

As Jenny and Zack pulled out of Richard's driveway, they remained quiet for quite some time. Finally Zack broke the silence. "I guess you have your answer now, huh?"

Jenny nodded. "It appears I do." She looked out the window as all the quaint houses sped by, wondering if any terrible secrets were contained within those walls as well. "I feel awful for him," she added. "He seems like he has a good heart."

"Agreed."

"Could you imagine if your own father put you in that position at just seventeen?" She turned to Zack. "I just can't wrap my head around it."

"It was shitty, no argument from me," Zack replied. "And I guess Brian knew it, too, offing himself just a few months later. I guess he couldn't live with what he'd done."

"Nope." Jenny reflected silently for several minutes. "I can't believe how many lives Luther Whitby ruined just because he didn't want his daughter to marry a poor man."

"Well, it sounds like Brian Larrabee did a pretty good job ruining some lives, too."

Jenny didn't reply.

"But do you know what's cool about this?" Zack looked mischievously at Jenny out of the corner of his eye.

"Oh dear."

"I'm still related to a murderer." Jenny snorted as Zack continued. "Now, I'm not his direct descendent or anything, which does knock the badass level down a few notches, but he was still a Larrabee."

"You're demented," Jenny posed. "And incidentally, in what universe is your grandfather's cousin your uncle?"

Zack laughed. "I was hoping you didn't catch that. I had no idea what to call him. Mr. Larrabee seemed too formal, but Richard seemed too casual. Before I knew it, 'Uncle Richard' just came out of my mouth."

"I guess now that I know the explanation it makes sense. You're forgiven."

"Thanks, boss. You know, I've got to admit, we made a pretty good team back there."

"You think?"

"Oh, hell yeah," Zack replied emphatically. "I was like the warm up guy. I got him warmed up with all that construction talk. And then when it came time for all that sensitive stuff, you took over." He held up his hand. "I've got to be honest; I would have had no idea what to say to him once he started crying. I don't do that well with tears, especially not a grown man's."

"Ovaries," Jenny replied. "People with ovaries can handle tears. It's part of that second X chromosome."

"I wouldn't know. Me, my penis, and my Y chromosome are too busy working construction." Zack's mood quickly switched to solemn. "You know, I'm actually pretty bummed that this is over. This was so cool. A nice little break from the norm."

Jenny thought about the whole experience—the people she'd met, the arguments it sparked, the atrocities she'd witnessed—and realized she wouldn't have changed a thing. "Yeah. It was pretty cool."

Suddenly she became much more alert and turned to Zack. "You know what I can't figure out, though?"

"What's that?"

"Why would I hear the name Arthur Larrabee when the shooter was actually Brian?"

The following morning Jenny sat across from Bill Abernathy at his desk in the police office. "But Richard had no knowledge of it," she concluded. "All he knew was that he moved some drums for his father in the middle of the night. He knew he'd done something that probably wasn't on the up and up, but he had no idea he was disposing of a body."

Bill shook his head. "I have no intention of pressing charges. Don't worry about that."

Jenny smiled.

"So, now that the case is officially closed, let me go get you Steve's things." Bill got up from his chair.

"Thanks, Bill." Jenny looked around nervously as Bill disappeared around the corner. She'd never been in a police station before, except for a field trip in the fourth grade, which hardly counted. She hoped to get out of the station before anything frightening happened.

Bill returned with the bags of Steve's belongings, placing them on his desk. "I think this is everything. We honestly didn't spend a lot of time going through it considering we pretty much had all of the details, thanks to you."

Jenny looked at the bags with a mixture of excitement and sadness. "Did you talk to Elanor about the funeral arrangements?"

"She said she'd take care of it," Bill replied. "I assume she'll follow through."

"I'm sure she will." Jenny gestured toward the bags. "So, do I need to sign for these?"

"No, ma'am, you can just take them."

With a deep breath Jenny shook Bill's hand, recalling how firm his grip was. "Well, thank you very much for getting these to me. I'm sure this will mean a lot to Elanor."

Back at the house Jenny sat on the living room floor with the bags spread out in front of her. After gathering her courage she opened the first bag, pulling out some trivial contents: silverware, dishes, and various other kitchen items. Next she removed an old framed picture—a black and white photograph of a stunning young girl sitting on a rock by a lake. She recognized that it was Elanor right away—she could tell by the eyes. Jenny remained motionless as she studied the image, marveling at both the beauty of the subject and the gravity of the find. She was mesmerized, unable to put the picture down for quite some time.

With a sigh she put the photo off to the side and continued searching the bags, finding mostly everyday items. She did pull out an envelope—a modern one—which she opened to find Steve's photo ID. Once again she found herself staring.

"So you're Steve, huh?" she whispered to the image. The picture on the identification card was that of a nondescript, light-haired man who Jenny could have easily passed on the street without a second glance. Fully aware of his character, Jenny felt immediate fondness for this man; she could see the kindness in his eyes. Her gaze shifted to the card's signature. Steve had signed this document with his own hand. He'd posed for the picture. He carried this very certificate with him in his wallet. A strange feeling of déjà vu washed over Jenny. "I'll just put you back in your little envelope," she said, nearly overcome with both familiarity and awe.

She continued to delve carefully into the bags, taking out each piece and deciding its importance. Most items seemed to be unsentimental; however, one particular item caused Jenny's jaw to drop.

Chapter 18

Jenny scooted the recliner closer to Elanor's bed so she could hear Elanor better. Elanor's soft voice reflected her exhaustion, and Jenny was having a difficult time making out what she was saying. "I figured it was all about the almighty dollar," Elanor said. "It usually is."

"I actually felt bad for Richard Larrabee," Jenny confessed. "He'd just been a teenager when his father asked him to do the unspeakable. It had clearly been weighing on him his whole life."

"That's terrible, to drag your kids into something like that. Especially when it's to get yourself out of a mess that you've created."

"Well, he apparently felt bad about doing it. He committed suicide a few months later."

"Did he now?"

"According to Richard he did."

"Well, I'll be damned. At least his sons got to live comfortably after that. If any piece of good news came out of this whole thing, it's that those kids didn't have to pay the price for their father's gambling addiction anymore."

"They do seem like a nice family." Jenny thought of Zack in particular.

Elanor gestured toward the bags at Jenny's feet. "So what do you have there?"

After a short pause, Jenny announced, "Some of Steve's belongings."

Elanor's eyes instantly opened wide. "Can you help me sit up, dear?"

"Sure thing, Miss Elanor." Jenny pushed the button to make Elanor's bed upright, pausing every few inches to help her scoot into the correct position. The oxygen tubes added extra challenge. As much Jenny hated the idea of losing her beloved friend, she also hated seeing such a vibrant woman reduced to this level of helplessness. In that regard, she almost hoped Elanor would go quickly.

Once Elanor was sitting comfortably, she eagerly asked, "What do you have?"

First Jenny pulled out the photograph of young Elanor. "I believe I might know who this is," Jenny said playfully as she handed the picture over.

Various emotions simultaneously appeared on Elanor's face. "He'd kept this picture on his table," she explained, never taking her eyes off the image. "I gave it to him." She caressed the frame lovingly, this being the first tangible piece of Steve she'd had in decades. After a moment she turned with as much excitement as she could muster and asked, "What else do you have?"

"I bought a frame for this, but I thought you might like to hold it first." Jenny handed Elanor Steve's ID.

Tears immediately flooded Elanor's eyes, causing her to laugh at herself. "I can't see," she giggled, blinking exaggeratedly. "It's the first time I can look at Steve's face in forever, and I can't even see it."

Jenny retrieved some tissues for Elanor, who dabbed her eyes. Eventually she looked back at the ID card and said lovingly, "Oh, there he is. Shit. I'm crying again." The tears of joy, sadness and laughter continued to stream down her face. She eventually closed her eyes and hugged the ID card in to her chest. "Oh, my beloved Steve." Elanor looked at Jenny through blurry eyes. "I can't wait to be with him again."

"I know you can't," Jenny said solemnly.

While dabbing her eyes Elanor asked, "Do you have anything else in that bag? I'm not sure my heart can take it."

"Just one more thing," Jenny said, producing a small black box. She handed it over to Elanor.

"Is this what I think it is?" Elanor asked bewilderedly.

"Open it," Jenny whispered.

Elanor opened the box to find a gold ring, enhanced with the tiniest speck of a diamond. Neither woman spoke as Elanor absorbed the intensity of the moment. She took the ring out of its box, placing it on the appropriate finger. She held up her hand like an excited new bride, inspecting it from various angles. "It's the most beautiful ring I've ever seen."

Jenny knew Elanor had probably never seen a diamond so small, but this ring represented the happiest time of her life. Countless hours of Steve's blood, sweat and tears paid for this ring, which to him must have cost a small fortune. "It's perfect," Jenny added sincerely.

"But it's too big," Elanor noted. "I've lost so much weight." She turned her hand downward, and the ring slid off onto the bed.

"You could put it on your middle finger," Jenny suggested.

Elanor laughed. "But I would flip everyone off every time I showed it to someone. *Hey, check out my ring. And by the way, fuck you.*" Elanor giggled again. "Too bad I like everyone here. Otherwise that could be useful."

"Yeah, I guess that's not the solution," Jenny confessed. "Besides, it's an engagement ring. It needs to be worn on the right finger. Hang on, I've got an idea. I'll be right back." After a disappearing for a short while, Jenny returned from the front desk with a roll of tape. "Here…we can add a little bit of bulk to the ring. Then it will stay on." Jenny wrapped the tape around several times until the fit was snug. "Is that better?"

Elanor smiled as brightly as her failing health would let her. "Much." She couldn't take her eyes off the ring. After a short while, she raised her tired eyes to Jenny and said, "Can you help me lay back down, dear?"

"Sure thing, Miss Elanor." Jenny helped Elanor lie back down with much the same difficulty and awkwardness she'd endured while sitting her upright. Once fully reclined, Elanor rolled over onto her side, placing her ringed finger in front of her face, admiring it as her eyelids began to grow heavy.

Jenny rubbed Elanor's arm. "Why don't you take a rest, Miss Elanor. You've had quite an exciting afternoon. And you were tired when I got here."

"I don't think I have a choice," she said with a weak giggle. "My body is crapping out on me."

"Well, go ahead and sleep." Jenny's tone became mischievous. "I can see myself out."

Elanor quickly drifted into sleep, but rather than leave right away, Jenny stayed in her chair and looked lovingly at Elanor. The end was inevitably near, and Jenny was well aware that any given visit could be the last. She wanted to drink in these moments while she still could.

Jenny smiled sincerely as she looked at the ring. The tiny diamond was endearing—a gift from a man who knew the promise was more important than the token. At that moment, a funny feeling took over her. Growing accustomed to the visions, Jenny was able to relax and become receptive to the message. She closed her eyes and found herself standing at a counter in a jewelry store.

"The lighting is so much better now," the woman behind the counter said. "And the fresh coat of paint makes such a difference. Thank you for doing all of that."

The same voice from the previous visions resonated through Jenny. "No, thank *you* for agreeing to barter with me. I tried to make this same arrangement with a lot of different stores, but they all told me no."

"Well, this works out for both of us. I needed work done. You needed a ring. We both benefit." The woman flashed Jenny a smile. "Sue is in the back getting it for you. I think you'll be pleased with how it turned out."

At that point a commotion caused Jenny to look over her shoulder. A young giggly woman was beaming as she held a giant diamond necklace in her hand, ready for purchase. Her other arm was wrapped around a man who was clearly twice her age but tried to mask that fact with over-the-top black hair dye.

Jenny knew that man. She recognized him from the picture at the sub shop. It was Arthur Larrabee.

Arthur locked eyes with Jenny, looking like a deer in headlights. Jenny had met his wife before; this was not her.

Jenny wordlessly turned back to the jewelry store employee who received the ring from her coworker. The woman opened the ring box, showing Jenny what was inside. "Do you like it?" she asked.

Jenny looked down at the ring which, sixty years later, would finally adorn the finger of the woman for whom it was intended. "It looks great. Thanks."

Then, as quickly as it had come, the vision vanished.

"Dear God," Jenny whispered to herself at Elanor's bedside. "Do I have this all wrong?"

Chapter 19

Jenny dialed Zack's number as soon as she exited Elanor's building. "Luther Whitby may not have done this," she proclaimed the second he picked up the phone.

"What?"

"Luther Whitby," she repeated. "He may not have been the one who paid off Brian Larrabee. It may have been Arthur after all."

"What makes you say that?"

"I had a vision. Just now," Jenny couldn't speak fast enough. "Steve figured out that Arthur was having an affair. That just might have been reason enough for Arthur to want Steve out of the picture."

"Get out."

"Yeah…with a sweet little thing half his age."

"This shit just keeps getting crazier and crazier. Who knew my family history was so scandalous?"

"Kind of gives you a whole new perspective on the old peoples' table at the reunions, huh?"

"Hell yeah it does."

Jenny went through the motions of entering and starting her car with her cell phone on her shoulder. "So how will we know which one was behind it?"

"Uhh…" Zack remained silent for a long time. "You're the psychic, you tell me."

Jenny started on the familiar route home. "I've got nothing."

"I guess all we can do is wait and see if Steve gives you any more insight."

"What if Steve doesn't even know who it was?"

"Then we probably won't either."

Not the answer Jenny wanted to hear.

"I need to meditate," Jenny said to herself after she hung up with Zack. "Where can I go that's peaceful?" Home certainly wasn't the place; even though Greg wasn't there, they had no comfortable furniture. Then it hit her: Lake Wimsat. There'd be no better place in the world.

She pulled into a store parking lot, typing Lake Wimsat State Park into her phone. She went in and bought herself a few things to eat and drink, and then she was on her way.

At the park she found a nice picnic table near a patch of trees. While it was hot, the combination of breeze and shade made the temperature somewhat bearable. She nibbled at the grapes she'd bought from the store and tried to quiet all the noise that perpetually cluttered up her brain. With a few deep breaths, she felt a layer of stress melt away.

"Okay, Steve," she whispered. "This is it, my friend. We're running out of time if you want to give Elanor answers. I'm ready for you, baby. Fire away."

Jenny closed her eyes, resting her chin on her fists on the table. Soon enough she was able to see Arthur Larrabee materialize in front of her, sitting behind a large mahogany desk in an elaborate office. "About what you saw the other day," Arthur began. He paused, waiting for a response from Jenny that never came.

He laughed nervously. "What were you doing in a jewelry store out in Braddock, anyway?" Arthur posed. "There are plenty of jewelry stores closer than that one."

Jenny folded her arms across her chest without a reply.

Arthur got a playful look on his face, clearly trying to appeal to the bond guys often share. "Well, I guess you know my dirty little secret now, don't you? But she was quite a looker, wasn't she? Old Arthur's done pretty well for himself." He smiled proudly, but that smile faded when he noticed Jenny didn't react.

He cleared his throat and continued. "I know it looks bad." He fidgeted in his chair. "But Marguerite's been impossible to live with lately. She's so fucking moody. She can be nice one minute and then be a bitch the next. I never know what to expect from her. It's like living in Hell."

Again, no response from Jenny.

Arthur's discomfort grew more apparent. "And she doesn't put out anymore. At all. If I didn't get some on the side I'd be getting it five or six times a year. A man can't be expected to live on that. You understand that, don't you, son?"

Silence.

Arthur leaned forward across his desk, reducing his voice to a whisper. "Surely a virile young thing like yourself gets where I'm coming from. I know you're fucking Luther Whitby's girl. He told me last weekend. He asked me to find a reason to fire you so you'd be forced to leave town."

While Jenny felt her insides grow hot, she remained outwardly stoical.

Arthur sat back in his chair, placing his palms dominantly on the table. "I don't have to find a reason to fire you, you know. I can keep you on the payroll forever. And you don't have to go telling anybody what you saw in the jewelry store, either. You get what I'm saying?"

Nothing.

"In fact, you might even deserve a raise for all that hard work you've been putting in." He gave Jenny an exaggerated wink.

No reaction.

Clearly, suddenly, Arthur's patience ran out. "Listen, you little fucker." Arthur once again leaned forward, lowering the volume of his voice, but this time in anger. "I am a very important man in this town. I can buy and sell half the people in Evansdale. I will not have my reputation ruined by some little piece of shit, dime-a-dozen construction fuck like you. You will keep your mouth shut, do you hear me? Or mark my words, I will have you ruined."

More silence.

Arthur put his finger in Jenny's face. "You think about what I'm saying, O'dell. And don't you breathe a word of this to anybody or you'll be sorry. Now get the fuck out of my office."

Jenny got up to leave, heading toward the door, turning at the last minute to note, "Maybe your wife is acting like a bitch because she knows you're fucking other women."

Jenny walked out the door of his office.

164

Slowly the sounds of nature took over Jenny's ears, the heat of the day once again feeling oppressive against her skin. She opened her eyes, concluding her vision, feeling both enlightened and confused at the same time. Two men. Two motives. One outcome. "What exactly took place all those years ago?" she whispered, looking around, wondering if Steve himself even had the answer.

Chapter 20

Jenny heard the door close downstairs and an immediate, "What the fuck?"

Greg was home.

Jenny braced herself for a second and walked nonchalantly down the stairs. "Did you have a good trip?"

"Where is all of our furniture?"

Jenny tucked her hair behind her ear. "Well, do you remember a couple of weeks ago, there was that apartment fire on Columbia Avenue?"

"Yeah." Greg was seething.

"One of the families there lost everything. They had no renter's insurance, and they have two little kids."

"And..."

"And I gave our furniture to them."

"God damn it, Jenny, I thought we agreed to sell the furniture."

"We didn't agree to that."

"Yes," Greg said impatiently, "we did."

"No, we didn't," Jenny replied calmly. "You said you wanted to sell the furniture, and I said I wanted to donate it. We never came to any resolution."

"Then why did you donate it?"

"To prove a point."

"The point being...?"

"That you always assume we're going to do things your way. For once I've insisted on doing things my way, and look at how you're reacting. You're acting like I've done something wrong."

"You gave away our furniture while I was away for the weekend. You don't consider that wrong?"

"Not under the circumstances, no."

"You didn't even check with me."

"What would you have said if I did?"

"I would have said we can't afford to give it away."

"Exactly," Jenny said. "That's why I didn't check with you."

"I can't believe this," Greg said with disgust. "I haven't even gotten through the door yet and already I'm dealing with this shit."

Jenny sat down on the stairs and lessened the intensity of her tone. "Greg, I've been doing some soul searching while you've been gone. I really think we need to see a marriage counselor."

"We can't afford one. You gave away our furniture, remember?"

Despite her disgust, Jenny remained calm. "Can you please stop fighting with me for a second and have a meaningful conversation?"

"You'd like that, wouldn't you? You give away our furniture behind my back and then you want to not fight about it. It doesn't work that way Jenny."

Jenny rubbed her eyes. "We are clearly not going to resolve anything here. We are at an impasse, and I think we need an objective third party to listen to us and let us know which one of us is being reasonable."

"I can tell you which one of us is being reasonable."

Brick wall, Jenny thought, *It's like arguing with a brick wall.* "So are you willing to go to a counselor?"

"Depends. How much is that going to cost us?"

"It's cheaper than a divorce lawyer."

"Ha!" Greg sneered. "That's an empty threat if I've ever heard one. You would never file for divorce."

"You know what?" Jenny said softly. "You're right. Second-grade-teacher-Jenny from Kentucky never would file for divorce. But psychic-Jenny from Georgia would. In a heartbeat. So I'll ask it again. Are you willing to see a counselor?"

"I'll think about it."

Once again, Jenny thought, *he feels like the decision is his.*

"Look what I have," Jenny said cheerfully as she approached Elanor's bed. She was holding up her recently-purchased *Choices* magazine and making it dance around.

Elanor smiled feebly. "Oh, a *Choices*. You *are* reading them."

"Yup," Jenny proclaimed. "Sure am. And, I'm going to fill out this little subscription card in the middle so I never miss an issue."

"I'm so glad to hear that. Not only do I hope it will toughen you up, but I hope it reminds you of me."

"Oh it will," Jenny said enthusiastically. "On both counts."

Elanor looked so frail in her bed. Jenny's heart was breaking, but she didn't want to let Elanor know that.

"Do you have any exciting news for me today?"

Jenny considered telling Elanor the latest development but thought better of it. Elanor was at peace with the way things were. Jenny didn't want to raise any questions that Elanor wouldn't live to see answered. "Nope. Just a visit." Jenny twisted her face. "Actually, I've come to ask you a question."

"What is it, dear?"

Jenny let out a sigh. "I remember when you were talking about Steve you mentioned that you knew it was love because it always felt like home when you were with him."

"That's right."

"Well, with Ronald and Mike…how did you know it was wrong?"

Elanor thought quietly for a moment. "For me it was indifference," she confessed. "At least with Mike, anyway. With Ronald I knew it wasn't right from the beginning. He was just a toy I was playing with." Elanor snickered. "Oh, God, isn't that awful? I have to be careful or I'm going straight to hell."

Elanor still managed to make Jenny laugh.

"But as dear as Mike was to me, I could easily picture him in the arms of another woman and it didn't bother me. In fact, the image of him making googly eyes at a woman who was madly in love with him made me happy. I wanted that for him, and I knew I couldn't provide it. Anyway, I guess it isn't normal for a woman to be able to picture her boyfriend with another woman and not be bothered by it. I think that's how I knew."

Jenny gave those words a little silent thought.

"Does this have to do with your husband?" Elanor asked softly.

Jenny nodded slightly. "Yes ma'am."

"I'm sorry to hear that, honey. I remember being in that situation, and it's a terrible place to be," Elanor said compassionately. "Oh, the mental tug-of-war I had going on before I broke up with Mike...Is this the right thing? Is this the wrong thing? Will I regret it? Oh, it was awful."

"But it was your indifference that ultimately made you decide to go through with it?"

"I think so," Elanor said. "It was hard, though, because I couldn't really give a good reason why I was indifferent. The best I could come up with was 'It's just not there.' Was that really a reason to break up with someone? Or was that just an excuse to avoid the scary prospect of marriage? It was so hard to tell."

"But I guess you didn't regret your decision after you did it."

"No, I didn't," Elanor said. "Mike deserved better."

"Unfortunately it's not my husband's well-being that I'm worried about," Jenny confessed. "I can't sit here and say that I have his best interest at heart. It's my own I'm concerned with."

"And that's a problem because..."

Jenny laughed at being called out again. "I'm not used to doing things that are that selfish."

"Insisting on being happy isn't being selfish. It's necessary. And it's not like the minute you stop being a doormat you instantly become a bitch. There's a whole big gray area between doormat and bitch. That's the healthy place you should strive for."

Jenny gave Elanor's words a little thought. "But it's true, actually. I guess I feel like if I make demands I *am* being a bitch."

"I don't think you could ever be a bitch," Elanor surmised with a yawn. "You don't have it in you. Your biggest concern going through life will be to make sure you stay out of that doormat range. I think your first inclination will always be to give too much, and you're going to need to constantly remind yourself not to do that."

"Well, I did just pull a stunt that might have been a little bitchy."

"Atta girl," Elanor said. "What did you do?"

Jenny explained the episode with the furniture. "So was that bitchy?" Jenny shook her head and added, "I can't believe I'm using the word bitchy."

"A little vulgarity is good for you," Elanor said. "It cleans the soul. And, maybe what you did was a little bitchy, but you have to take into account the circumstances leading up to it. It's not like you just randomly pulled that stunt. That would have been bitchy. But Greg himself admitted that he wouldn't have agreed to it if you'd asked, so you were just doing what you needed to do." Elanor nestled into her pillow and closed her eyes. "Besides, in what universe is donating furniture to a family who lost everything considered bitchy behavior? Not my universe."

That notion hadn't occurred to Jenny before. Her husband was making her feel bad about being charitable.

And he could only make her feel bad if she allowed him to.

While Jenny wanted to keep the conversation going, she had to recognize Elanor's waning energy. "Why don't you take a little nap, Miss Elanor. I won't leave while you're asleep. I'll just hang out here and watch a little tube, unless the noise will keep you awake."

"No, it won't keep me awake," she muttered sleepily. "Jackhammers to my head won't keep me awake these days."

"Okay, then," Jenny said compassionately. "Sleep tight."

Elanor fell asleep almost instantly, and Jenny made herself at home with the television. She propped her feet up in the recliner and flipped through the channels until she found a mindless comedy rerun. A little unsophisticated humor was just what the doctor ordered at that moment.

She found her mind drifting aimlessly during the commercials. Also feeling a little tired, Jenny closed her eyes only to find herself looking at a blurry rendition of the half-built house on Meadowbrook Road. Though the detail was difficult to see through the haze, the house looked a little further along than it had been during the vision of Steve's shooting. Clearly this was a short time after.

A man paced around nervously in the front yard. Jenny floated in closer to get a better look at who it was. She strained with all her might, trying to get the best glimpse possible, finally deducing that she was looking at a frazzled Brian Larrabee.

A car pulled up to the desolate cul-de-sac, and a man wearing a hat emerged from the car carrying a bag. This second man approached Brian, greeting him with a handshake. Jenny tried desperately to determine who he was, but the image was too blurry.

The gentlemen exchanged words, but Jenny could hear only sound. The second man handed Brian a bag, which surely contained reward money for making Steve disappear. If only Jenny could make out who it was, she'd have her answer. She zoomed in closer, trying to make out the features of this mysterious second man. Finally, one trait made itself abundantly clear.

Black sideburns.

It was Arthur Larrabee. Jenny felt elated that she got her answer, but just as her spirit began to soar, another car pulled into the cul-de-sac.

A figure materialized from the car, also holding some sort of bag. The figure approached Brian, also handing over the bag, also giving Brian's hand a shake. Jenny circled the trio, looking for some identifiable features on this third man. Knowing him better, she was more easily able to identify who he was.

Luther Whitby.

Jenny swirled through the air as she watched the three men interact for a few moments. Soon she saw Arthur and Luther drive away, leaving Brian by himself in the barren front yard. Brian dropped to his knees, holding his head in his hands, clearly remorseful for what he'd done.

Unlike at the scene at the lake, Jenny made no attempt to silently console the man on Meadowbrook Road. She merely watched, unfazed by his regret, feeling as if he deserved every ounce of guilt he was harboring. He, along with his heartless wealthy friends, had ruined everything for Steve in the name of greed and ignorance.

"Was the money really worth it?" Jenny wondered. She could think of nothing material that could have possibly justified what he'd done. "Prisoners," she thought to herself. "Prisoners of a society where people measure themselves by what they have."

The noise from the television once again became audible, signaling to Jenny the vision was over. She opened her eyes, finally content that she had solved the mystery once and for all. Which of the two assholes had paid off Brian Larrabee?

They both did.

When Elanor finally woke, Jenny disclosed the latest findings from her two most recent visions. Elanor nodded in response, signaling to Jenny that she understood, but still seemed too tired to react in any other way. She drifted off to sleep again, and after another hour Jenny decided it was best to leave. Unable to say goodbye in person, she left a note taped to Elanor's bedrail.

"Good morning, sleepy head. I figured I'd let you sleep—it seems like you need it. Thanks for your advice today. I'll definitely take it to heart.

"I won't be able to come by tomorrow; I'm going to start setting up my classroom. I will be by the day after that, though. In the meantime, get some rest. Love, Jenny."

In the car Jenny called Zack to inform him of her latest visions. He was at work, so the conversation was brief, but he concluded by saying, "So do you think this is really it? No more curve balls?"

"God I hope not," she declared. "I don't think I can take much more."

Chapter 21

Jenny looked around her classroom approvingly, admiring the way the decorations were falling into place. The woman who had retired the year before left all of her materials behind, giving Jenny plenty to choose from. She decided to decorate each wall by subject; English and math were complete, and next was social studies. Jenny thumbed through pictures of presidents, maps of the explorers' routes, and replicas of important documents, trying to determine which images were worthy of display.

This was Jenny's favorite time of the year, academically speaking. She always loved those last few weeks of summer where she could come into the school and set up her classroom at her own pace. Once the actual school year started, things always became so hectic that the days went by in a blur. Late summer, however, was relaxing and peaceful.

Suddenly Jenny was overwhelmed by a flood of emotion. A rush of excitement generated through her, followed by a joy so intense it brought tears to her eyes. She felt warmth and happiness; her entire being was utterly consumed by love. After the initial surge, fear gripped Jenny when she realized what she'd just experienced.

Reunion.

Jenny immediately grabbed her purse and ran out of her classroom. She darted into her car and drove to Maple Estates as quickly as she could, but the drive seemed to take an eternity. Finally she arrived, rushing through the sliding double doors which had preceded so much happiness in the past. This time, however, the doors invoked a miserable sense of dread.

Jenny approached the familiar desk in the lobby, attempting to be casual. "Hi, Stephanie," she said to the woman behind the desk. "I'm here to see Elanor again."

Stephanie's face looked glum. "I'm sorry, Jenny, but Elanor passed away about an hour ago."

While the news wasn't a complete surprise, it was still difficult for Jenny to hear. Tears flooded the back of her eyes, but she blinked them away. "Okay," she said with a false sense of strength and acceptance. "Well, thank you very much." She turned and immediately headed out to the parking lot, hoping her tears could wait until she reached the privacy of her car.

Once inside, the tears fell freely. She covered her face with her hands and sobbed. Elanor had been such a wonderful person—one of the most important figures in Jenny's life. They had only known each other for a short time, but the bond was deep, and Elanor was the person Jenny felt closest to in this new town she called home. She was going to miss the visits—miss the chats.

Jenny was going to miss her friend.

Jenny walked slowly into the house where Greg was, not surprisingly, hard at work. He looked at her strangely as she approached him, sensing that something was terribly wrong. He didn't ask in words, but his quizzical look invited an explanation.

"Well," Jenny began solemnly, "it looks like you have your wife back. Elanor passed away this morning."

"Oh," Greg said. "I'm sorry."

She knew he wasn't.

She walked past him and sat in the solitary folding chair in her living room. The house's emptiness was a tangible reminder of Elanor's kindness, which Jenny would never be able to enjoy in person again. Elanor had provided Jenny with so much—insight, companionship, confidence—what was she going to do without her beloved friend?

She looked around the disheveled house, realizing that this was the only facet of her life now. Assuming Steve would cross over since he and Elanor had reunited, there would be no more of the contacts she'd grown to anticipate. Jenny's life, which was briefly exciting and enjoyable, would once again seem unfulfilling. She was just Mrs. Greg Watkins again, home renovator and fourth grade teacher. She lowered her head into her hands and sobbed.

As Jenny walked through the entryway of the funeral home, she stopped at every photograph of Elanor on the series of display tables, studying each picture copiously. The earliest photos revealed an impeccably-dressed and happy child, sometimes alone, sometimes situated between her parents. Jenny glared intently at the man who ultimately caused so much pain to so many people, wishing silently to herself that he was burning in hell.

She noticed how beautiful Elanor's mother had been, just as Elanor had described. She regarded the elegant house, which she now owned, in the background, standing majestically, unaware of its future decline. For a moment she was grateful for Greg's desire to restore the structure to its original grandeur; she just wished he could have been a little more reasonable about where that restoration should fall on his priority list.

As Jenny continued along the tables, she watched Elanor age into a beautiful young woman. The pictures of a teenage Elanor were plentiful, yet Jenny noticed the absence of photographs from Elanor's penniless days. The images resumed once more, but only when Elanor was already in the throes of the magazine. Most of the pictures featured Elanor hard at work, oblivious to the camera, making sure the magazine achieved her impossible standards.

One picture featured Elanor dressed elegantly, standing arm-in-arm with a man in a suit. Based on the age Elanor appeared to be in the picture, Jenny surmised the man had to be Mike. She studied him admirably, recognizing what a decent man he was, sympathizing with the fact that he unwittingly engaged in a competition he could never win. Jenny smiled at his image, hoping that wherever he was he could sense her approval.

The pictures progressed, moving from black-and-white to color, Elanor's hair advancing from blond to gray. Jenny noticed that there were no pictures featuring Lake Wimsat, proving to her that the person who chose the pictures didn't really know Elanor that well. Anyone who knew her intimately would have known to include such an image.

Jenny rounded the corner to where Elanor's body was featured, surrounded by flowers, in the front of the room. Folding chairs served as pews; most were empty. Jenny didn't recognize any of the people that were there, but she gathered from overheard conversations that the guests were mostly business associates and distant relatives. Jenny took a seat for the moment, not inspired to associate with these people who didn't bother to visit Maple Estates. They probably eased their consciences by sending obligatory Christmas cards each year, but they also allowed a fascinating woman to die alone in a nursing home. *I was her only true friend,* Jenny thought. *The only one who bothered to get to know the woman behind the magazine.*

Jenny eventually gathered the courage to approach the casket, kneeling at Elanor's side to say her final goodbye. She viewed the shell of the woman in front of her, lying peacefully with her fingers interlaced, looking nothing like the woman Jenny once knew. Her features appeared different, and her beautiful blue eyes were closed, masking the spark that was distinctly Elanor. The discrepancies made the task of paying her final respects easier; it almost seemed she was saying goodbye to a stranger.

"I know you're happy," Jenny whispered. "I know you are because I felt it. I know you're with Steve now, where you belong. Your pain is over. You're free of the body that was failing you. I know you are in a better place. But I will miss you." Jenny wiped the tears from her eyes. "I feel selfish for being sad, but I am. You've come to mean so much to me. I'm going to be so lonely without you. I'll miss all of our little talks. But I'll take what you've taught me to heart, Miss Elanor. I promise I will. I'm a changed woman, thanks to you. You can take comfort in knowing the granddaughter-you-never-had now has a brighter future in front of her. I owe that all to you." Jenny once again wiped her tears. "I truly do love you, Miss Elanor. I know I'll see you again one day. Just behave yourself until I get there, okay?" Jenny smiled, taking one last look at the lifeless body that she knew no longer contained Elanor's spirit. She stood up from the perch upon which she had knelt and once again sat alone in a folding chair.

She saw Nancy Carr come in and make small talk with some of the other guests. Eventually Nancy approached Jenny and had a brief conversation, consisting of conventional pleasantries. After a short time Nancy continued to circulate, once again leaving Jenny alone with her thoughts.

"Is this seat taken?"

The voice was familiar. Jenny looked over her shoulder and exclaimed in surprise, "Zack! What are you doing here?"

Zack sat down next to Jenny. "I came to pay my respects," he replied. "From what you said, she sounded like one hell of a lady."

Jenny's heart soared with gratitude and affinity. "Thank you," she said, "That's very sweet of you."

"Well," Zack added, "my family kind of ruined her life. It's the least I can do."

Jenny shook her head defensively. "Your family changed her path, certainly, but they didn't ruin her life."

Zack held his hand up apologetically. "I didn't mean to imply her life was ruined…"

"I know," Jenny said quickly. "I'm sorry. I just…" Jenny didn't know how to finish her sentence. As tears filled her eyes again, she looked as Zack and said weakly, "She had a great life, you know?"

Zack nodded, looking uncomfortably down at his lap. "It sounds like it." The silence that followed was awkward; Jenny remembered how Zack felt about tears. The notion caused her to smile.

"Well," Zack began with a glance toward the casket, "I guess there's no time like the present." He stood up out of the chair and said, "Lightning isn't going to strike me up there or anything, is it?"

"Why would it?" Jenny asked.

"I'm a Larrabee. She may not want me anywhere near her."

"Elanor Whitby of all people knows not to judge someone by their last name."

Zack held up one finger. "True." He headed up to the casket, kneeling down and lowering his head.

Jenny watched him up there, looking out of place in his suit, bidding farewell to a woman he'd never met. All in all, Jenny concluded, Zack was a good man. In so many ways he was the opposite of Greg. He was able to feel compassion for a stranger. He was willing to help, simply because it was the right thing to do. Most importantly, however, he bothered to come to the funeral. Her own husband couldn't pry himself away from light fixtures in order to be there for her. Zack, a virtual stranger, cared enough to come.

Zack returned to his chair, looking remarkably unfazed. He held on to his tie as he sat back down, turning to Jenny. "I guess you were right. No lightning."

"Of course not. She would have liked you," Jenny remarked. "I'm sure of it."

At that point the priest called everyone to attention so he could conduct the service. He was an articulate man, delivering an eloquent eulogy that would have made Elanor proud. Jenny felt satisfied that appropriate homage was paid to her dear friend, although she wished more people had been there to hear it.

Since Elanor's wish was to be cremated, there were no additional services scheduled. Most guests left the funeral home in groups, talking casually about matters that didn't concern Elanor. Zack and Jenny walked out side by side, although not a word was said between them.

Once they reached Jenny's car, she looked up at Zack, squinting in the sunlight. "Thanks again for coming." Her voice began to crack. "It means a lot to me."

Zack cleared his throat and looked around. "Yeah, no problem."

Jenny knew the tears made Zack uncomfortable, but she couldn't help it. As they flowed freely down her cheeks, she wiped them away with the back of her hand.

"I feel like I should hug you," Zack mumbled, "but I know you're married and I don't want to make your husband mad."

Jenny snorted. "Everything I do lately makes my husband mad. Besides, he doesn't have the right to say anything. As far as I'm concerned, if he really gave a shit, he'd be here with me. But he's not. You are."

Zack pulled Jenny in for a hug that was a little too long and a little too tight, but somehow felt comfortable and right.

Jenny initiated the release. She couldn't bring herself to make eye contact with Zack, but she did admit, "Thanks. I needed that, actually."

"That's what I'm here for."

The silence was awkward. Technically this should have been goodbye. Now that the murder had been solved, Zack and Jenny had no reason to get together unless the motive was personal. Jenny wanted to say something about staying in touch, but she wasn't sure whether that was appropriate given the circumstances. All she knew was that she didn't want him to leave—not at that moment, and not from her life.

Jenny had to admit that a piece of that initial attraction was resurfacing. More tears began to flow as Jenny considered what a terrible mess her life was becoming.

"I don't want to leave you like this," Zack said. "Are you going to be okay?"

"I don't know," she admitted honestly. "I don't know much of anything anymore—except that I don't want to go home."

Zack shrugged with one shoulder. "We can go get a coffee or something." As an afterthought he added, "Between friends."

Thoughts stirred around her head. Was it appropriate for her to accept? Greg would have been furious if he knew. Even she had to admit this may have been considered crossing a boundary. Fortunately or unfortunately she didn't have the energy to care about that. She was at the bottom of the emotional barrel, and coffee with Zack was the only idea that seemed even remotely appealing. Was she about to put another nail in the coffin of her marriage? Perhaps. Would some of her friends back in Kentucky lose respect for her if they found out she'd done this? Most likely. Did she give a shit?

No.

"Coffee sounds great," she said. "Do you mind driving? I don't think I'm in any condition to."

"No problem," he said smiling. He touched his hand lightly to the small of her back, guiding her in the direction of his car, causing a tingle inside Jenny. She knew this was bad news. She was playing with fire. And she couldn't have cared less.

As she headed toward Zack's car with his hand on her back, she saw Nancy Carr looking in her direction. Jenny knew she must have looked like a deer in headlights, but Nancy only smiled politely and continued on. *It's just coffee,* Jenny thought to herself. *Among friends. Nothing to be ashamed of.*

Zack opened the passenger door for Jenny and she climbed inside his car. After he walked around and entered the driver's side door, he commented, "Did you see that chivalry? That was awesome, huh?"

Jenny had to laugh. "Very impressive."

"See? I'm learning."

"Your waitress friend should be impressed," Jenny added, disappointing herself with her own words. She had nearly forgotten that Zack had had his sights set on another woman. Perhaps Jenny was simply fooling herself into believing an attraction was there. Her already low spirits sank a little further.

"Incidentally," Jenny continued, pretending to be unfazed. "There's a little matter of gas money to settle. According to my calculations, you only have one day left to get gas money out of me, unless you've asked her out already and you're just holding back."

"No, I haven't asked her out," Zack confessed. "You might as well go out and buy yourself a shirt or something. I don't see you owing me anything."

As they headed out of the funeral home parking lot, Jenny asked, "Chickening out?"

"No, I'm not chickening out. I just don't think I'm going to ask her out anymore," Zack kept his attention focused on the road.

"Why? What happened?" Jenny had to admit a small part of her was happy.

"Circumstances have changed. She's not as attractive to me as she used to be."

Jenny looked at her lap. Those words invoked excitement, fear, happiness and confusion all at the same time. She knew she was going to have a lot of thinking to do once she became strong enough to face it. At that moment, however, she didn't have that strength.

Shortly they arrived at a coffee house and logistical matters took over. Once they had their drinks and were seated at a booth, the more serious conversation resumed.

"I hope you don't mind me saying this," Zack began, "But I'm surprised to hear you and your husband are having problems. I just assumed you were happy."

Jenny wrapped her hands around her coffee cup. "No, I'm not happy."

"What's wrong?"

Jenny found herself having a difficult time saying the words, unsure of whether or not it was proper to disclose her marital problems to a man she might have been interested in. However, nothing romantic had happened between Zack and Jenny at that point; as far as anyone was concerned, they were nothing more than friends.

Jenny gave Zack a brief description of the issues she and Greg had been having. "It's not like we were once a happy couple and now we're in a rut," Jenny concluded. "I'm beginning to realize our relationship has never been good. I may have never even loved him. I think I may have just loved the way I felt about myself when I was with him."

"Wow," Zack remarked, blowing on his coffee. "That's pretty heavy."

"Too heavy," Jenny agreed. "Except now I'm stuck. I took a vow. I can't just walk away."

"Well, you *can...*"

"I know I can. Technically. But that's not something I take lightly." Jenny covered her eyes with her hands. "Can we talk about something else?"

"Sure," Zack said. "Pick a topic."

"Okay," Jenny replied with a sigh, sitting up straighter. "If no one could tell you no, and money was no object, what would you be doing with your life?"

Zack repeated the question quietly as he thought. "I would have a boat, and I would be out on the water almost every day."

"What about in the winter?" Jenny asked.

"You're not good at fantasizing, are you?" he asked. "You said money was no object, so I would just go to the Caribbean or something."

Jenny had to laugh at her own practicality. "I guess that makes sense."

"So what about you?" Zack asked. "What would you do with all that money?"

"Mine's dumb," Jenny confessed.

"Let me be the judge of that."

Jenny smiled shyly. "I would use that money to live off of and become a professional psychic."

"That's not dumb," Zack replied. "That's like the coolest thing ever."

Jenny felt herself blush.

"I'm serious," Zack continued. "If I had that ability, I'd do the same thing. I think it's so cool that you can do that." He leaned forward on his elbows. "So what does it feel like when you have a vision?"

Jenny shrugged. "It doesn't feel like anything. It's like I'm living it, but I'm just standing still with my eyes closed." An epiphany hit Jenny. "Did you ever have a very realistic dream, and then you wake up surprised to find out that you're actually in bed? It's kind of like that."

"What about the voices?" Zack was enthralled.

"It's just like listening to you right now. In fact, the first time I heard a voice I thought it was my husband talking to me." Jenny's heart sank when she became reminded that she was married.

She quickly forced that thought out of her head. "But the coolest experiences were the visions from after Steve had died." Jenny described her vision of Elanor and Ronald at the lake in detail, as well as her most recent sighting on Meadowbrook Road. "I think that's what things look like after you die…before you cross over, that is."

Zack put his hands on his head. "This is so wild. Do you realize that you and I know something that most people desperately want to know but don't? I feel like one of the most important people in the world right now."

Jenny laughed at his excitement and awe. He had the zeal of a child.

"And your husband really doesn't think this is cool?" Zack asked. "I can't imagine that. It's like he hit the jackpot and he doesn't know it."

Jenny shrugged modestly. Perhaps she *was* married to the only person in the world who didn't value her ability.

"I bet you could make a living out of this," Zack said. "People would totally pay you to contact their loved ones."

"That's just it," Jenny replied. "I don't contact their loved ones…their loved ones contact me. And so far, only one person has done it. Maybe he's the only one who ever will. This may have been a one shot deal."

"That would suck."

"That would indeed suck," Jenny confirmed. "Especially if I quit teaching and tried to do that for a living."

"But if other people do contact you, would you quit teaching?"

"If I could," Jenny reasoned. "The problem is that even if this did happen again, I wouldn't make any money at it, unless there was a reward or something. I'd still have to teach to pay the bills."

"Bummer."

"I know…especially if someone contacts me while I'm at work. I can't just walk out in the middle of class because I'm being pulled somewhere."

"Pulled somewhere?" Zack asked excitedly. "What does that feel like?"

Jenny sighed as she thought about it. "Automatic. Like if you're driving a route you've driven a million times before, you can still get where you need to go, even if you're thinking about something else. It's like I just know where to go, except the path is unfamiliar. I become somewhat trancelike, and the car finds the way."

"I'm so totally jealous," Zack marveled.

"Be careful what you wish for," Jenny found herself saying.

"You don't like being psychic?"

Jenny twisted her face. "It's not that I don't like it; it's just the visions don't always come at a convenient time. And they're not always pleasant. I actually felt Steve get shot."

"See, though, I think that's cool. How many people actually know what it feels like to be shot?"

Jenny cocked an eyebrow at Zack. "There are some things I can go through life without knowing."

Zack leaned back in the booth. "I don't know. I still think it'd be a cool thing to know."

"Would you like me to shoot you?"

Zack laughed. "No. I'm mortal. I'd have to heal. You get to get shot and not be hurt by it."

Jenny snorted at his word choice. "I'm still *mortal*. Something's going to get me one of these days."

"I bet it will be worry."

Jenny made a face. "You're probably right."

"So," Zack switched gears abruptly. "What happens now?"

"What do you mean?"

"What happens now? Like, do you and I say goodbye and never see each other again?"

Jenny lowered her eyes and spoke softly. "I hope not."

"Well, I've been thinking," Zack continued cheerfully. "You're renovating a house, and you may need some help from time to time. I figure you could call me if ever you need an extra set of hands. I worked in the field for years, remember. I know a thing or two about construction."

Jenny smirked. "I thought you hated it."

"I do," he confessed. "But I can deal with it for a friend." He flashed a sincere smile at Jenny.

"Okay, then. Here's my end of the bargain," Jenny proposed. "If ever I get contacted again—by someone other than Steve, I mean—I'll call you, and you can help me work on the case."

"You'd do that?"

"Of course. You were absolutely instrumental in solving this one."

"That's awesome," Zack announced proudly, "I can be your sidekick."

"Partner," Jenny corrected. "There are no sidekicks."

"It looks like we have ourselves a deal." Zack extended his hand across the table, and Jenny shook it.

"Deal," she said with a smile.

Elanor's lawyer, the executor of her will, contacted Jenny with some details about the spreading of the ashes. The funeral home would be releasing the remains within a few days, and Jenny would be given both Steve's and Elanor's ashes in a scattering urn. "The will says you know where to scatter them," the lawyer stated.

"Yes, sir, I do." She truly didn't know, but she was confident she'd be shown the way.

"In addition, at your leisure I'd like you to come by my office. There are a few things Ms. Whitby wanted you to have."

Jenny smiled at the prospect of receiving something to remember Elanor by, besides the furniture which would eventually wear out. She believed she'd be getting her painting back, but perhaps there was something beloved of Elanor's she'd get to keep. She decided at that moment that she'd take one of Elanor's mementos, as well as one of Steve's, and she would put the items together in a small memorial in one of the spare bedrooms of her home.

"I can come by today," she said, "If that's okay with you."

"Can you be here at four?"

"Sure can," Jenny replied.

"That's great," the lawyer said, "I'll see you then."

Jenny entered the lawyer's office promptly at four, informing the secretary of her arrival. She waited as instructed in the lobby, brimming with excitement over what Elanor may have left for her. After what seemed like an eternity, Jenny was called back into the office, where she was greeted by a lanky, well-dressed man. "Andrew Parker," he said, extending his hand.

"Jenny Watkins."

"Have a seat, Ms. Watkins," he began, gesturing to the chair across from his desk. "Now, before I begin, I want to let you know that what you are about to receive is not officially part of the estate. All of those items have to go through probate and may take a while before they get released. As you know, Ms. Whitby's estate was quite large."

"Yes, sir, I can imagine."

"Some of these items I give you today were rightfully yours, according to her, and she's just giving them back. Other items were *presents*, in her terms." He made quotes with his fingers. "Considering the relatively small financial value of these items, I don't believe they'd be challenged in probate."

Jenny smiled. "Yes, sir."

He reached back behind his chair and grabbed two handled bags, placing them on his desk. "This first bag had her personal effects from her room at Maple Estates. She wanted you to have them, saying that some of those items had been gifts from you in the first place."

"That is true, yes." Jenny was excited to be getting Steve's belongings back.

"Oh, including this," Andrew said, reaching back one more time for the meadow painting. "She said you made this."

"Yes, sir."

Andrew looked at the canvas. "That's very impressive."

Jenny blushed. "Thank you."

"The second bag is the gift bag from Elanor. She had paid one of the nurses from Maple Estates to go shopping for on her behalf with a very specific list of items she wanted you to have."

Jenny smiled at the notion. She could see Elanor giving the nurse the instructions in her own feisty way. Jenny's smile faded as she realized she was never going to witness Elanor's spunk first hand again.

"Well, thank you so much," Jenny replied. "This really means a lot to me." She stood up to leave.

"Wait one more minute," Andrew said, opening his desk drawer. "She did leave you a portion of her estate in her will."

Jenny's eyes widened. "She did?"

"She sure did," Andrew replied. "Now, like I said, an estate this large has to go through probate to see if anyone is going to contest the will, but in the meantime I do have a check here for you with a small portion of your inheritance. This should be enough to tide you over until probate is finished." Andrew handed her a sealed envelope, which Jenny took in disbelief.

"Let me help you out to your car," he continued as Jenny still struggled to grasp what was happening. "I'll take the bags," he said. "I'll let you carry the painting. I wouldn't want to scratch it."

Jenny mechanically went to the car, placing the items in the back seat. She shook Andrew's hand and said goodbye, climbing into the roasting vehicle. As soon as Andrew was back into the building, Jenny opened the envelope and looked at the amount of the check.

"Holy fucking shit," she exclaimed. "One hundred thousand dollars?"

Jenny didn't want to be bothered by Greg as she went through the sentimental items Elanor had left her. Instead she stopped in a parking lot, left her car running for the air conditioning, and climbed into the back seat of her own car.

She first opened the box of tokens from Elanor's room. There she did find the old photograph of her on the rock, as well as Steve's framed ID card. The engagement ring was noticeably absent. It appeared Elanor had kept that, which made Jenny happy. That ring was Elanor's; it should have gone with her to the grave.

In the second bag she found some high-quality paint brushes, countless colors of oil paints, and a two hundred fifty dollar gift card to a craft store. Tucked in the side of the bag she found a sealed envelope with very shaky writing on the outside, simply saying *Jenny.*

Jenny quickly opened the note, eager to discover what her dear friend's last sentiments were for her. On a simple piece of loose leaf paper, Elanor had scribbled out her final goodbye.

Dear Jenny,

If you're reading this, I'm already with Steve. I know that's where I am because of what you have told me. You have made me so happy, you have no idea. I want you to enjoy that same happiness in return, so here are some painting supplies. For the love of God, PAINT. You're great at it, you enjoy it, and I don't want to hear any excuses. PAINT, dammit!

Jenny put the note down for a second as she laughed and wiped away a small tear. With a deep, invigorating breath she continued.

I have also left you some money, and I want to be very clear about what I want you to do with it. I know you are a very generous and giving young woman, but I want you to keep most of this for yourself. Don't worry, I have already left plenty to charity. That's taken care of. This money is specifically for you so you can live the life you were meant to lead.

I want you to pursue your gift. Give answers to people, just like you did for me. Enrich lives. Do what only you can do. While I firmly believe that teaching is an admirable profession, you weren't meant to be a teacher. You were chosen for something more. Be that person that you were chosen to be.

You have given me more than anyone ever has, with the possible exception of Steve. In return, I hope I have made you realize that no one can tell you no. And now money is no object, so you can truly go and live the life you were meant to lead.

I love you with all my heart, and I take comfort in knowing I'll see you again someday. No hurry on that. Get old first.

Until we meet again,
Elanor

Jenny held the letter close to her chest for several moments until she found the strength to read it again. The second time the letter was just as impactful as the first, if not more so.

This letter had just changed her entire life.

When Jenny arrived home, she was able to face Greg with a new outlook. She was no longer stuck in the marriage, forced to stay due to financial obligations. She only needed to stay with Greg if she wanted to, and that was going to be difficult to determine.

Aware that she had taken a vow, she did feel that she should make every effort to help her marriage survive. Upon seeing Greg working very hard on his hands and knees in the formal living room, she felt a sense of guilt for the way things had been unfolding. He was working hard for them; she had to at least give him that much.

"Hey," she said softly.

"Hey."

She sat on the floor near where he was working. "Have you thought any more about that counselor?"

Greg sat back on his knees. "I'm just not sure we can afford it."

Jenny curled her legs into her chest. "The way I see it, we can't afford not to."

Greg and Jenny looked at each other silently for a moment, and then she continued.

"Elanor has left me some money. I'd like to use that to pay for counseling."

"How much money?"

"I'm not sure yet," Jenny confessed, "but it's a lot. I got an advance of a hundred thousand dollars, and the lawyer called that a *small portion.*"

"Are you serious?"

"The check is in my purse. I'll deposit it tomorrow when the banks are open."

Jenny could see the wheels turning in Greg's head. Before he got ahead of himself, she decided to speak her peace. "I don't want to work on this renovation anymore," she said softly. "I will help with paint schemes and wall hangings, but I don't want to rip up floors and replace pipes. I figure we can use some of Elanor's money to hire a competent person to come in here and help you on my behalf. In fact, one of the guys at Larrabee homes said he'd be willing to help if we needed it, and that was before he knew he'd get paid."

Greg didn't say anything, so Jenny kept talking. "And I'd like to resign my post at Evansdale Elementary. There are still a few weeks before school starts, and I know there were more applicants than positions. Somebody else will be delighted to have my job instead of being a daily sub."

Greg looked confused. "Then what will you do? If you don't work here and you don't teach…"

"I want to be a full-time psychic."

Greg's expression changed instantly. "You know I don't like you disappearing all the time."

"I know," Jenny said sympathetically. "That's one of the things we're going to have to work through. But I *am* going to be a psychic. The question is whether we're going to stay married while I do it."

Greg remained quiet for an eternity. "I guess we'll need to see a counselor, then."

Chapter 22

The next day Jenny received a phone call from the funeral director, inviting her to come by and pick up Elanor and Steve's ashes. Jenny obliged, meeting with him later that afternoon.

The funeral director opened the box on his desk, presenting Jenny with the wooden urn inside. "It's an avian urn," he explained. "Once the ashes are scattered, the urn itself becomes a bird house. That's designed to represent the continuation of life."

Jenny smiled as he delicately placed the urn back into the decorative box. Providing a family of birds with a home seemed characteristically Elanor.

He slid the box across the desk to Jenny. "Thank you," she said graciously. "And thank you for the beautiful service."

The director smiled. "It's the least I can do for such an iconic woman."

After an overly-cordial goodbye to the funeral director, Jenny carried the box containing the urn uneasily out the door. She arrived at her car, grimacing, unsure exactly where to put the box. The trunk seemed cruel, but the passenger compartment seemed creepy. "Okay, lovebirds," she whispered, "I'll put you in the back seat. But no hanky panky back there, got it?" She placed the box on the floor of the car, wedged safely between the front and back seats.

She climbed into the front of her car and spoke more freely. "Alright, guys, you need to be quick about this. I'm not going to drive around like this forever. I'm giving you a week, and if you don't show me the way, I'm winging it. You got that?" She looked around the car in every direction, making sure if Elanor and Steve were there she'd have sent a glance their way. She started her car and headed home.

The following morning, Jenny was in the middle of her bowl of cereal when a sudden urge made her realize breakfast needed to wait. She didn't even bother to tell Greg she was leaving; she simply collected her purse and headed out the door.

Realizing this was most likely her last contact from Steve, Jenny savored the moment. She would miss his presence in her life almost as much as she would miss Elanor. She allowed herself to be driven to Lake Wimsat, a path she would soon be able to recognize without assistance.

Once in the park, she headed down the windy main road, past the facilities maintenance building, to a small parking lot that could have easily gone unnoticed. Aware this was her destination, she pulled the car into one of the slots.

Stepping out of the car, she looked in the direction of the lake, noting this area was even more overgrown than the area behind the facilities maintenance building. "Seriously?" she complained to herself as she pulled her boots out of the trunk. Once her boots were on and the urn was tucked safely under her arm, Jenny headed out into the thick brush.

After what seemed like an eternal hike through vines and pricker bushes, Jenny finally arrived at a large, flat rock that jutted out into the water. She remembered Elanor had once described this place, but the description hadn't done it justice. Jenny was awed by the beauty that surrounded her, instantly understanding why this had been Elanor and Steve's favorite place in the world. She was glad this was going to be their final resting place. Together. Just as it should have been.

Jenny took a seat on the rock, unwilling to bid her final farewell just yet. She placed the urn next to her, pretending for a moment that Steve and Elanor were young and very much alive, sitting with her in a moment of comfortable silence that only the closest of friends could enjoy. They could have been friends, the three of them, had the stars lined up differently. Unfortunately it wasn't meant to be.

"Oh, Elanor, I could use you now," Jenny said out loud as she considered the prospect of her failing marriage. No longer bound by financial chains, the choice was hers as to whether she wanted to stay or go. She was grateful that Greg had agreed to go to counseling, but she was smart enough to know that counseling could only be effective if both people involved genuinely wanted the marriage to work. She wasn't sure if that was true for her. Part of her wanted to cut her losses and go.

She heeded Elanor's advice and tried to picture Greg with another woman. She envisioned him looking longingly into her eyes, whoever she was, making promises similar to the ones he had made to Jenny in the beginning. She felt frighteningly unmoved, but she was fully aware that may have been because this was only a theoretical relationship. Perhaps if the real thing had been flaunted in her face she'd have felt much differently. Unfortunately, that was one of those things she wouldn't be able to discover until it was too late.

Switching gears she tried to determine whether she'd be interested in Greg if she'd met him at this point in her life. Did he have the qualities she was currently looking for? She didn't think so. Did Zack have those qualities? She didn't really think so either, but she at least enjoyed his company. She couldn't even say that about Greg anymore. She did believe there was a man out there who was much better suited for her than either of those two, but was she fooling herself? Did the perfect man really exist?

"I want a Steve," she declared.

Lying back on the rock with her fingers interlaced over her stomach, Jenny spent her final moments with Elanor staring up at the sky considering the pros and cons of divorce. Jenny sighed out of frustration. The only way for her to know the correct solution would be to choose an option and then determine if she regretted it later. The safer option was to stay married; she could always file for divorce down the road. If she filed for divorce, that was final. Greg would probably never agree to take her back if she took that step. Staying married was definitely the safer route.

But was it the route that would make her the happiest?

Jenny turned her head toward the urn and repeated, "Miss Elanor, I really do need you. I wish you were still here. Will you give me a sign, at least? A little help? Something? *Anything?*" She waited for a moment for something to happen, but nothing did.

With a sigh Jenny sat up, realizing she was selfishly keeping Elanor and Steve from being together in their final resting place.

They'd been waiting for decades; she didn't need to make them wait any longer.

She stood up carefully, picking up the urn and admiring it. "Well, you two," she whispered softly. "I wish you an eternity of happiness. Godspeed, my friends, until we meet again." She tilted the urn, and the ashes flew like dust into the gentle breeze. Jenny watched until she couldn't see any remnants of the ashes left.

And just like that, they were gone.

In an effort to sidetrack herself from her sadness, Jenny directed her attention to what was now just a beautiful wooden bird house. "We'll have to find a nice place for you," she said thoughtfully. Then she added, "Dear God, I'm talking to a bird house."

With a sigh she headed back through the jungle to her car, where once again she exchanged her boots for her flip flops. As she got into the car, she realized this chapter of her life was now over. However, she was hopeful the future would be brighter than the past.

Jenny got home and fixed herself some lunch, eager to busy her mind with other things. After making herself a sandwich, she headed to the folding chair in the living room, balancing a plate on her lap. She noticed the issue of *Choices* on the floor next to the chair, so she picked it up and opened to a random page. There, staring her in the face, was an article entitled, "Fear Is Not A Reason."

Fear is not a reason.

She could hear the words as if Elanor's own voice had said them. *Fear is an excuse,* Elanor would say if she could. Jenny wondered if Elanor was actually hovering nearby, wishing those words into Jenny's brain. Jenny had asked for a sign, after all. Perhaps this was it.

At that moment Jenny decided she would make educated decisions about her future, not at all motivated by fear or baggage. From that point on, Jenny would make conscious, deliberate *choices.*

Two months later:

Jenny sat at the edge of Lake Wimsat with her easel and paints, recreating the beautiful scene of the water surrounded by autumn's foliage. She had indeed surrendered her teaching job to a grateful college graduate who had previously accepted the fact that she'd been overlooked by all the school districts. Jenny had regarded that as a happy ending for everyone concerned.

By this time Jenny had been made aware of the amount of money Elanor had left her; she would undoubtedly be comfortable for the rest of her life. She had received another installment of her bequest, and she decided to use part of it to give some tokens of appreciation to Susan and Zack. She knew that without their support, she never would have been able to give Elanor her answers. She found it only fitting to show them her gratitude by sharing some of Elanor's generosity.

She had set up college funds for each of Susan's children. Unless the kids decided to go somewhere ridiculously upscale, Jenny's trust should have adequately covered all of their expenses. Susan was moved to tears when Jenny gave her the gift, although she did joke that she'd been doing this for thirty years and had made only a fraction of what Jenny managed to pull in with her very first experience. The two women vowed to keep in touch, and they had since gotten together several times.

Jenny presented Zack with a new boat, aptly named the *Elanor O'dell*. She had paid for a docking space at Lake Wimsat so Zack could enjoy the same peace and beauty Elanor and Steve used to enjoy. Zack had jumped up and down like a child when he saw the boat, a reaction which still invoked a smile in Jenny every time she thought about it.

She and Greg had several counseling sessions under their belt, but she wasn't horribly optimistic about their future. She realized that most of the reasons to stay in the marriage were fear-based, and she now knew that fear was not a reason to stay.

She had also been seeing a counselor of her own, separate from the marriage counselor, to get a handle on her inadequacy issues. She was continuing to make breakthroughs and progress, but she understood she had a long way to go. Just as Elanor had made discoveries until the end, Jenny realized self-reflection was a never-ending process.

As Jenny sat back in her folding chair—the one that had served as their living room set until the furniture came in—she admired her half-completed painting. She'd changed the colors of some of the trees, putting in reds where yellows had been. She was giving herself permission to do such things lately and discovering she was usually happy with the result. This painting was no exception; she liked how it looked so far.

At that moment a strange wave hit Jenny. It had been a while since she'd experienced it, but she immediately knew what it was.

Contact.

To be continued in *Betrayed.*

Made in the USA
Middletown, DE
12 May 2022